HENRI LEAG

No Stars

Victor Wolff Book 1

For my sisters.

1

Victor checks his bow-tie in the reflection and straightens it.

The hanging lamps over the mirror bathe him in golden light as he takes a final look at his tux. *You can tell a lot about a person by the way they dress*, he reminds himself. It's something he was taught early on in his work. People will believe anything if you're dressed right.

He doesn't let a trace of dust interrupt the microscopic frays of his expensive black velvet tuxedo, laced with gold to go along with the theme of the event. Gold, so precious once. Gold meant power. Not so precious now that there are *other* ways to gain power. Power, the most valuable resource in the universe.

The golden-rimmed mirror seems to agree with him, his reflection staring back at his clean-shaven face, slightly discolored by night life and work. Satisfied, he smiles and pulls the door back after taking in a quick breath. It still excites him, this moment, when his hand is on the door handle, on the threshold. He doubts he'll ever feel that feeling fade.

He opens the door and a vastness of noise wraps around the silence of the restroom. Victor Wolff strides out with his hands clasped loosely behind him, back straight, shoulders back, and a sideways smile.

The party dances across the room. An orchestra plays away

at an inspired waltz. Men in black and gold dip their silver-dressed ladies as they move around the room in a synchronized ballad.

Victor crosses the ballroom, careful not to step on any dresses, his shiny black shoes clicking against the floor to the rhythm of the music. So many smiles. He can't help wondering how many are fake. How many of those smiles are really trembling lips hoping for an end to the fake-happy. Wondering when the real-happy starts.

He didn't come for the ball, though. Victor crosses over to the sitting room. The contrast between the two rooms is like the contrast between light and shadow. There's no dancing in the sitting room. No real smiles here. It's *all* fake happy.

Victor takes a look around the room. The light is different here, brighter, sharper, almost blinding in the reflection of the golden and silver dresses. All around, there are people who blend in perfectly in the painting of a jazz-era comedy. And then there are the ones who are completely out of their element.

Like the little boy standing in his way, staring at a corner of the room where a little girl about the same age is sitting in a golden dress. Victor fights to suppress a smile and kneels down to the boy's height.

"Who's that?"

"Huh?" The boy looks startled.

"You should go talk to her."

The boy blushes and walks away crestfallen.

"Or not."

Before he can stand back up, he sees a woman, silver-dressed like all the others and hair tied back in a tight bun, picking up her purse with a gloved hand. Completely out of her element. And she's staring straight at him, almost glaring. There's a certain keenness in her green eyes, as if she's searching for someone, someone who doesn't want to be found.

And then she's gone. He sees the tail of her dress disappearing behind a door.

A waiter comes around with a tray of drinks. "Champagne, sir?"

Victor comes back to himself and takes one of the glasses, "Thank you."

The waiter nods and starts walking away.

"Actually, do you have a list of guests?"

"I'm sorry, I'm not allowed to share, sir."

And the waiter moves on to offer champagne to two men listening intently as a third forms an imaginary gun with his hands, taking aim in Victor's direction. Their tailcoats make them look like huge penguins.

Victor moves closer, stepping in between the two penguins. He waits to interrupt, "You sure know how to throw a party, Mr. Hunt," Wolff says, raising his glass.

Mr. Hunt replies cautiously, "Thank you, uh—?"

"Victor Wolff, sir."

"The lawyer?" He chuckles, a phlegmy sound with a guttural growl behind it, "Boys, this young man is Adolf's right hand, his top lawyer."

"I'm a consultant. I talk less than a lawyer." Victor corrects politely.

Mr. Hunt hesitates, "I don't suppose you're here for drinks, Mr. Wolff."

"I never turn down a party," Wolff smiles.

"Right." He turns to the other penguins, "I'll be back, boys, keep the waltz going."

Hunt leads Victor down a hall. Through a window, he catches

a glimpse of the gloved woman, just as she walks to the stairwell. Then the door shuts behind him, and he finds himself in a study.

The lights flicker on with a lower glow than the ones in the sitting room. Victor walks over to the enormous window in the place of the fourth wall. Clouds surround the building but he can still see small, blinking lights dancing across the city below. Tiny cars and little people are no more than microscopic dots from where he's standing. It gives him a vague sense of flying and vertigo. The penthouse takes clear advantage of the increased atmosphere on Urbis, taking the skyscraper past the barrier of the clouds. Rain would never stain these windows.

"Would you like a drink?" Mr. Hunt's deep, booming voice pulls him out of his trance, but he doesn't let it show.

"I'm not old enough to drink, I only took it to be polite," He says, shaking the still full glass in his hand, watching the champagne lose its bubbles by the second.

Mr. Hunt turns, surprised, "You look old enough. How old are you?"

The word nineteen slips through his mind, but it's not something he likes to share. "Not old enough to drink."

Mr. Hunt shrugs and pours himself a glass. He sips a quarter of his drink down and looks back up. His tailcoat is straight at the shoulders, but it tightens around the bulging arms. The remains of his liquor stain his orange whiskers. Hunt smooths a hand over his tightly groomed hair, raises his glass, with a maple-colored liquid in it, "Champagne is for parties. And like I said, you're not here for the party, are you?"

Victor doesn't answer. He knows what a man struggling to buy time looks like.

"To business, then." Hunt sighs.

Victor smiles to himself, *This is where the fun begins.* His smile curves into a loose smirk as he straightens and lowers his drink onto the table. "Mr. Hunt, that drink in your hand, how much did it cost?"

The entire situation runs a chill up his spine. He likes starting like this, starting a seemingly harmless conversation, like a boxer putting on his gloves. And he talks quietly so Hunt has to lean in. Someone once told him his voice is like a whisper through a megaphone, quiet, but everyone will listen.

"How much do you make?" Chuckles the penguin.

"A lot for talking." Victor smiles back, "How much do *you* make?"

Hunt's smile fades. "Enough."

"Including Mr. Wren's money?"

Hunt slams his glass on the table, sending it shaking, and points a big forefinger at Wolff, "What are you getting at, Wolff?"

Victor flinches no more than the slightest movement of his hand. He slips it in his pocket. "I'm giving you your only chance, Mr. Hunt." He starts walking slowly around Hunt's chair.

The man retreats his finger, but he still looks like an orange cat ready to pounce. "You think I'm dumb enough to trust you?" The words are fierce, but they can't mask that unmistakable twitching of the mouth, the dilation of the pupils. Fear. This is Victor's favorite part. When the hunter becomes the hunted, and he becomes the Wolf who corners his prey. The moment where he holds all the power, the most valuable resource in the universe.

"Mr. Hunt," he continues, "You have two doors. Behind one of them is me, your friendly neighborhood consultant. Behind the other is Mr. Wren. You have a debt now, you see. I can help you pay off said debt if you give up your share in the Newton Project."

And there it is. The rain becomes a storm.

"You think I would give up my most lucrative endeavor?" His eyes are twitching now, "Tell Adolf I'll pay off the debt, but that's it."

"This debt is a little too big. And I wouldn't recommend getting on Mr. Wren's bad side. He has means of getting what he wants."

"I'm sure you can show yourself out." He doesn't bother to stand up, just takes his glass and takes another sip. The last of the liquid drains into his mouth.

Victor walks past him and steps out into the hall. He looks back to see Hunt, hands in his pockets, looking out the window into the night sky. Victor shuts the door and walks out of the penthouse into the elevator. Just as he's turning, a man runs into him, excusing himself. Victor ignores him, he's too deep in his own thoughts to care or even notice.

That hadn't been as fun as he thought it would be. This was always his least favorite part. It was a rare occasion when he could not convince a client to go his way, but there were always stubborn goats who would rather risk death than lose money. Lose power. Now it's Wren's turn with them. A pang of guilt surges through Victor's body. That pang of guilt never leaves. It's always in there, somewhere distant.

The elevator doors slide open, and the bustling night life of Urbis welcomes him as he walks out of the building. A long black limousine pulls up to the entrance and a skinny, toad-eyed chauffeur pops out of the front and opens the door for Victor. His lip quivers slightly, and there's a layer of gleaming sweat on his forehead.

"Everything alright?" Victor asks.

The chauffeur doesn't answer.

Victor cautiously steps into the limo. The door clicks locked as a hand pushes the barrel of a gun to the driver's temple, making him gulp.

Victor shrinks back and reaches into his coat. He grits his teeth when he feels the mag-less gun in his pocket.

"Drive." Says the man with the gun, his voice rougher than Victor expected. The car starts and growls silently into the street.

"Where are we going?" Victor asks.

"You don't need to worry about that." The man is staring straight at him from behind the driver's cap he took from the chauffeur's head.

"Are you a hitman? Someone sent a hitman after me?" It almost makes him laugh.

"You don't need to worry about that."

"'Course not, why would I?" Victor groans, tossing his gun to the floor of the limo.

They've been driving for half an hour now, and the shadow of a tall narrow building grows like a weed at the eastern edge of the city.

"You work for Crow?" Victor asks the hitman.

No answer. Instead, the hitman takes Victor by the collar and tells the chauffeur to wait outside. He shoves Wolff all the way to the top floor. The elevator opens directly into a room furnished like an office. Two chairs in front of a desk and a bookshelf on either side of the room, symmetrically drawing the leading lines to the end of the office.

A stick-thin man with a goatee stands to receive him, he signals for the gunman to retreat.

When, he had gone, the man points to one of the chairs.

"You must forgive Jerry," He says with a strange accent from some other planet, "He's a bit paranoid." This was meant to be a joke, but he said it with such a lack of emotion that the silence could have made the dead uncomfortable. "Please, sit."

"I won't be here long." Victor recognizes this man from the news and a few other gatherings. The blue eyes, slick black hair, and overbite smile showing only upper teeth all belong to Norton Crow, the owner of the *second* biggest company in the system.

Clearly uncomfortable, Crow nods, "You know who I am?"

"I've dealt with some of your clients." Victor keeps the calmness which got him his job. A smile escapes him for a split second.

"Yes, it seems you have. It's my clients who have told me about you. They say you're quite the consultant."

No response.

"Alright, straight to the point then. I want your services, how much does Wren pay you?"

"I've been asked that question extensively today."

"I'll double it."

"The question? I think once is enough, thanks." He says it almost automatically while scanning Crow's face carefully. His curiosity is aroused. *What could be worth so much money?* He wonders.

Crow lets out a short, desperate laugh which makes Victor think of the fake-happy people at the party. This guy is the king of fake-happy. "No, the money."

"Out of pure curiosity, what would I have to do?" He notices

Crow's jaw tighten.

"Wren. I want him out of the game—"

"I'm not a hired gun."

Crow leans in, "I don't need him dead. I want everything he's built to crumble like the shaky foundation it was built on. I want him to *watch* as his empire falls."

Victor leans in to match him, "*Why?*"

It's almost a whisper, but it drives Norton Crow back into his chair. He straightens his hair, "If you want the job, I'll pay you half now, half when it's done."

Victor sits back, "You brought me here at gunpoint against my own will, not even a warning, to tell me that you want my boss to go down in flames, and you think I'm about to sell out for twice my wage?" Wolff turns to leave, but Crow calls him back.

"Your boss isn't worth your loyalty. He's a swindler! You think his money comes from his company? If you knew half of what I do, you would be running away as fast as you can. His 'underground business' runs much deeper than interplanetary transport and logistics, Mr. Wolff."

Victor had heard these rumors before, but he'd never given them much thought, he isn't about to start, but he decides it's worth asking, "What underground business?"

"If I knew, I would have been in my grave long ago. But you know all about that, don't you?"

The sound of the words out loud chill through Victor's bones. His fists clench.

"If you don't know that, how can you know there is one? Underground business?"

Crow hesitates a long time. For a moment, Victor thinks he might've lost his voice, but then, "My wife knew. She found out." There's a strong crack in his voice, "She *is* in her grave. He took all I had. I want him know the half of how it feels... Did you know her?"

Victor tries to be sympathetic. "I knew her. She was there when Mr. Wren hired me. She was nice."

"Yes, she was. And now she's gone. And I want her *back*." The words drain the air from the room til Victor thinks he might suffocate. "You have no idea the things your employer has done, Victor."

Wolff casts his eyes down. Like a bullet with his name on it has just been shot at him, a knife with a reflection he recognizes. He pushes the feeling down. "I'm sorry, I can't help you." He stumbles against himself to get to the elevator. The doors slide open and he suddenly finds himself staring at his own eyes in the mirror.

"Please, Victor! He made my daughter believe *I* did it! You have to help me!" His voice echoes with desperation.

Wolff stops himself from crossing the doors.

"He took my Marilyn." Victor sees Crow in the mirror sitting with his forehead dropped into his open palms. But he looks up at a quick utterance from Wolff.

"I'll do it."

Crow gulps down a sob and breathes roughly. "Thank you. Thank you! She's—"

"I know who she is." Victor steps into the elevator, his reflection mimicking him, questioning him. "I'll bring her back."

2

The words keep bouncing around in Victor's head, time and time again. What had he meant? The words had slipped out of his mouth, determined, then. But now they seem to carry less weight with every echo, like a scream lowered to a whisper, barely audible.

He hadn't waited for any further instructions, just walked into the elevator and let it drag him down to the ground floor where his chauffeur was waiting for him beside the limo with the hitman.

The driver opens the door with a shaky hand and loyally asks if "Mr. Wolff" is "quite alright".

"I'm fine, Hans," is all Victor can bring himself to answer. No witty remark. No charming grin. Just "fine".

Hans's small, almost whiteless eyes relax.

The hitman blocks his way into the limo and hands a card over to him. "We'll be in touch."

"Mhm."

"You've agreed, there's no backing out now."

Victor glares up at the hitman.

"Fine."

The hitman smiles and steps out of the way. Hans settles into his seat after shutting the door.

Victor sits quietly. At this point, he'd usually start a conversation with Hans, "How's your grandson?" or "How old are you, Hans?" But this time he doesn't know what to say. And he's afraid of saying anything.

"Sir," Hans is looking back at him through the rearview mirror, "Would you like me to call the authorities?"

Yes, please. "No. Thank you, Hans. I doubt that'd help." He swallows a knot in his throat as he says it.

"Yes, sir." Hans's graying eyebrows turn up in confusion. The glowing lights of the city color the window in neon and LED light and all fade away as the glowing gold of the Wren Citadel bathes the limousine like the sun at midday. The limo brakes in front of the door. The Citadel dwarfs Crow's cold, lifeless building in every sense. Bigger, shinier, newer. Better. And Victor walks in.

A sports game is playing on the television in the lobby. He's never liked sports, but it's not that kind of game. It's some sort of strategy game show. Checking to call your opponents bluff.

Victor looks away from the TV to check his watch. It's thirty minutes past ten and he's standing in the lobby watching a game show, stalling for time he doesn't have. He takes a breath and forces himself away from the door.

There's music playing in the elevator, some kind of electronic jazz. Playing to the beat of his pulse as the floors fall past him. He watches through the glass wall, counting. One. Thump. Two. Beat. Three. Pulse. Until finally the elevator stops. He can hear his own breathing over the music, and the doors slide open. Floor one-twenty-one.

The hall is darker than the rest of the building, but only slightly. A woman sits typing away at a computer on her desk.

Her eyes are so glued to the screen she doesn't even notice Victor come in until he clears his throat.

"Mr. Wolff?" Her eyes shift back and forth from him to her screen. "You're late."

Victor breathes silently. *Calm down*, he tells himself. *Never let them see your fear.* "You're still here."

She doesn't even acknowledge the comment. "He's waiting for you inside."

"Yeah." He mutters under his breath. "I thought so."

Never let them see your fear. He grips the handle.

But the door opens before he can go through. A narrow, lanky man steps through the door, dressed in velvet red and gold jewelry from the cuff links to the watch and rings with a letter *D* engraved in calligraphy.

He has a horrible smirk scribbled on his face.

"You must be Victor Wolff." He says.

"And you are?"

"My name is Michel Delune. I'm your replacement. Or I will be one day."

Victor scoffs. He doesn't have time for this. "Whatever you say, pal."

"Yeah, just watch out, first mistake you make and I'm stepping in, Vic. Watch your back."

"Sure thing."

The man just stands there. He doesn't move out of the way, like a bony wall. "I need to get through."

"I move when I want to move."

Victor would laugh, but there's something gripping his nerves and playing them like an out-of-tune harp. He just shakes his head, exhausted already. And he waits.

"That's what I thought." Michel Delune puffs his chest out.

And he moves aside. Victor feels the guy's eyes following him as he walks into the room. And he feels the smirk of the man whose name he's already forgotten trailing after him like an obnoxious shadow. A shadow he doesn't have time to acknowledge.

A tall, built man in his fifties leans over a stack of papers. He straightens and spreads his arms toward Victor. "Just the person I wanted to see. You're late. How've you been?" Wren takes him by the shoulders and looks at him fondly, smiling proudly.

"I've been good, Mr. Wren. Is that a new suit?"

Wren is wearing a dark gray pinstripe suit over a black shirt and red tie. His short hair is graying at the temples, but his eyes are keen on Victor. A vinyl is playing on a turntable behind him. And an old song buzzes with the static.

"Oh yeah, you like it? A gift. From our friend over in Bajir. A thank you for that thing you handled for him last year."

"Well, where's my suit?"

"Ah, don't worry about that, we got tailors all over the galaxy, I'll get you a suit from up in Luminoir. That's where they know how to make a suit right."

Victor nods. He doesn't know how much longer he can keep it up. And a piano riff plays in the background.

"You sure you're alright?" Wren asks. There's something more than just care in the sentence. Like he's asking, *Is there something you wanna tell me?*

Victor nods.

Wren scratches his chin and nods back. "You know, I love this song,"

Victor can't take it. But he nods.

And Wren starts humming,

"It's a world for the kings, Victor! It's our world." He laughs and swings slightly to the music.

But Victor can't find the voice to laugh.

Wren squints his eyes, "To business then?"

"To business."

"Alright." Wren sits on the edge of his desk and speaks into the telephone. "Dana, will you get Miss Finch in here for me." He looks back at Victor, "Always helps to have a secretary in the room."

Victor doesn't even look at the chairs in front of him.

"The boy who never sits." Wren grins.

"Well, you know how I work, sir. I'm better on my toes."

"Yeah, hand in pocket, slight grin, shoulders back. Tactics to—"

"To gain the power in the room." Victor knows very well that those tactics have become his regular stance.

Wren smirks and squints, fingering the letter opener on his desk. "Always be the most powerful person in the room, Victor. Remember that. It's always the guy with the gun people listen to."

A shiver runs through Victor's spine. He feels Wren's piercing eyes cutting through him, like a player on that game show, calling his bluff.

He feels a flood of relief when Wren's eyes finally shift away to the door. A thin girl with loosely-tied brown hair, about the same age as Victor, stands sliding the door shut behind her. She stops beside Wren holding an orange folder with a bunch of files shoved neatly inside. Her blue eyes scan over Victor with a hint of suspicion.

"Victor," She greets.

Wolff steadies himself before answering.

"Marilyn."

She smiles curtly and hands the folder to Wren, who takes no time to throw it open and flip through its contents.

"Well, Victor? Tell me about our client, how's he doing?"

"Unfortunately, stubborn. There's no shaking that guy. He says he'll pay what he owes, but he's not giving up the shares." His eyes keep shifting to the secretary.

Wren purses his lips and rubs his chin. "I guess even Mr. Wolff here can't win all of them, eh? You know, Miss Finch here has told me she doesn't approve of your methods. So what are our options here, Marilyn?"

Marilyn seems surprised to be involved, but she doesn't hesitate, "There are other ways to obtain the shares for the Newton Project. Mr. Hunt wasn't the only one with money in the project. If we get the others' shares, Hunt will have no choice but to surrender his own."

"Or go bankrupt." Victor mutters.

"Yes." Marilyn answers sharply. A gleam of something passes through her eyes. Sadness? Fear? Guilt?

Victor feels his hands shaking. The words pass through his head over and over again: *I'll bring her back.* Why? Why had he said it? His eyes rest on Marilyn. Again a shiver passes through him. He forces himself to look back at Wren. *Does he know?* He notices a hint of madness in Wren's gaze, but he can't decide if it's his imagination. Victor's stomach turns and he feels vertigo rise into his throat like he's falling through a dark hole flailing to find something to grab onto.

In spite of what he tells himself, he knows what happens to the clients he fails to convince. He knows how they disappear. He feels his fists clench. Wren is staring at him, suspicion darkening his squinting eyes. *You have no idea the things your employer has done.*

"Victor?"

Victor swallows down a dry throat. His breathing has quickened, it's all he can do to talk. "Yeah, I'm just thinking."

"The other shares, can you get them?" Wren's tone sounds grave.

Reluctantly, Victor answers. "I can get them."

"Good. Where's our next client, Miss Finch?"

Marilyn answers shakily, staring at Victor. "He's on... a cruise. To Egeria."

"Victor, Miss Finch will get you a ride. Anything else you need, just let her know. Whenever you get the shares, just—"

"Why doesn't Miss Finch come with me?"

The room gets quiet fast.

"What?" Wren laughs, "Why?"

Victor swallows a sigh, "Well, she doesn't approve of my methods, right? This is her suggestion, maybe her methods are better."

"No," Marilyn argues, "Mr. Wren, I'm not a consultant—"

"Well, like you said, sir. It never hurts to have a secretary in the room."

Wren leans back in his chair, watching Victor silently. Marilyn just gapes, eyes wide open. "Alright. Miss Finch, you don't mind going with Victor, do you?" His eyes don't move.

"O-of course...sir."

"Good, it's settled then. You can go, Miss Finch. Victor, stay."

Victor sees Marilyn glance back as she shuts the door. He turns back to see Wren crossing his arms. He reaches into a drawer.

"Don't leave without it, Victor." Wren slides something across his desk. The barrel of a handgun gleams menacingly. Victor picks it up, weighing it. It's fully loaded. "Your life might just depend on it." Wren's glare is like bullets shot out of the pistol. His eyes are like threats themselves.

Victor nods and walks away, still feeling the crushing gravity of the words. They follow him out of the building. Into the car with Hans. Into his dark apartment. Into his dreams. Nightmares. Fears. And the whisper echoing around his bedroom: *Never let them see your fear.*

3

The bedroom breathes with the gleam of the sun. Victor zips up his almost-empty luggage. He fingers the black-gripped gun. He has one of his own, but he's never had to use it. He keeps it locked in a safe, and he doesn't intend to take it out, but this gun feels different. It feels familiar, but it's not one of Wren's cheap bodyguard guns like the one he carries. He wraps his hand around the grip and sits on his bed, letting the morning sun wash over his face. He closes his eyes and takes a breath. But the gun sucks all the air out of the room. And his finger slides over the trigger.

He waited patiently for night to come, packing the last of his things, keeping the gun in his pocket. He figured he'd find a way to get it through into the boat. But he wouldn't let it get away from him.

It sits in his pocket rattling slightly with the hum of the limo gliding through the streets of Urbis. He sees Hans through the rearview. The driver seems to have forgotten everything that happened the day before. His eyes look surprisingly passive. Victor feels a rush of envy at Hans's forgetfulness.

Throughout the entire day, the turmoil had boiled into a horrible vertigo inside him, making him nauseous at the thought of running into Marilyn before the cruise.

He'd bought a suit at the tailor's. A quaint little shop owned by Hans's wife, comfortable and homey. He'd ordered a suit the night before, and miraculously Mrs. Hans finished it just in time.

Looking in the mirror, he had tried to repeat the words to himself, *You can tell a lot about a person by the way they dress.* But the words kept morphing into *Never let them see your fear.* But he could see the fear marked by lines in his face all the same.

"We're almost there, sir." Hans says to the rearview.

An enormous floating cruise ship hovers over the space port. A multi-tiered luxury ship filled with rich decor and rich people, all set to sail through the stars. Waves of people parade into the ship, looking up at the fireworks shooting from the deck, laughing with mouths curved into "ooh, ahh" shapes. All Victor sees are faces. Faces leaning in to hear each other as if they have something interesting to say. Some look pale green before even getting on the ship, eyes lost in their own anxiety.

Victor swallows down a dry throat as Hans parks and opens the door. *Just get the job done*, he tells himself, *then we'll see.*

Hans hands him his suitcase, "Your baggage, sir."

His baggage seems heavier now.

Victor pushes past the crowd to get somewhere near the front. He wasn't given special credentials or anything. Wren's name is all the ID he needs.

"Name?" A man with a beak of a nose pushes a hand out at Victor without bothering to look up from his clipboard.

"Victor Wolff, I'm here on behalf of Mr. Wren."

Beak-Nose takes a look at him and whispers something to his droopy-eyed companion, whose eyes snap open when Beak-

Nose turns back to Victor.

"Something wrong?" Victor tries.

Droopy Eyes brisks off into the ship.

"What's that about?"

"You can board, Mr. Wolff."

"Hey, what was that about?" But the man is already attending the next person in line.

Victor takes a final look at the crowd, craning his neck for a glance of Droopy Eyes. His foot almost slips at the edge of the ramp and he's left crouched down and staring at the black emptiness of the water crashing against the side of the ship. The sloshing makes him dizzy. He gently lifts himself back up and moves on to the safety of relatively dry floor.

The luxurious promenade stretches on with lines of jewelry stores and top-tier restaurants, ironically located at the bottom tier of the ship.

Victor makes it onto a bridge overlooking more shops and cafes, people dressed in fancy tailcoats and tuxedos like penguins. He looks down at his own suit. Overdressed seems relative when you look at some of the people on the ship, but tailcoats went out of style ages ago. *They're catching back on,* Victor rolls his eyes. He's grateful for his plain black tuxedo with a red bloom on his lapel. He feels overdressed.

Wolff walks away from the bridge and hears a shuffling behind him. Victor takes a hall to the elevators, the shuffling following him the entire way. He passes a silver vase full of flowers, catching the reflection of a man in a white suit and thin whiskers walking not far behind. He jumps into an elevator, where the man follows.

Wolff steadies his breathing into a rhythmic pattern. He's been tailed before. The man crosses his arms, revealing a pistol in his pants. The sight of a gun doesn't shake Victor.

The doors start sliding together. "You know what, I changed my mind." Victor slips through the slit in the closing doors. *Amateur.* The man flinches as the doors open back up. After a while, they slide shut on his blushing face.

The White Rose's menu is limited to so-called "fancy dishes" served on porcelain platters and a bed of edible flowers. It's dimly lit and full of two-chaired tables. But all in all, the risotto is good.

Victor finishes the last spoonful of risotto as the candle burns out in the middle of the table. It's just bright enough that he can see the faces of the people around him, all sick, mad, or madly in love with their shrimp cocktails.

The empty glasses of shrimp cocktail start to shiver as they clang together on the tables. Victor braces, watching his spoon rattle on the plate. The tables begin to vibrate softly. The floor sends a chill through Victor's spine like the bass at a concert mosh pit. He turns to the window to see people waving at the cruise ship, getting smaller by the second. And the city gets farther and farther away. And they're rising. And they're flying.

After a few minutes, the vibrations stop, and the silence morphs into laughter and a quiet engine hum.

A sudden worry hits Victor like a gut-punch. *Had Marilyn boarded? Did Mr. Wren smell the rat and change his mind?* He lets out a sigh, but a knot ties in his stomach. Then, the chair scrapes and Marilyn sits down in front of him.

"Mr. Wolff." She says, her light voice not showing a hint of worry.

"Miss Finch."

"You know how to dine. It took me a while to find you."

3

"Risotto." He points with his spoon.

"Have you talked to the client yet?"

"You should try it, it's good."

"Mr. Wolff, please."

"Apparently the shrimp cocktail's good, but shrimp doesn't agree with me. It's the tail I can't get past."

"What?"

"By the way, who *is* the tail?"

"Victor, can we get to business?"

"I don't recognize him. Probably some temp or intern."

"A tail?"

"You look nice."

"What are you—"

"Thanks." Victor signs the check and gets up with Marilyn following behind him.

"Victor."

"Yeah?"

"Where are you going?"

"Ice cream."

Marilyn sighs and follows him to an old-diner-style ice cream shop.

"You want anything?" Victor asks.

She rolls her eyes and orders. Victor takes a spoonful of his cheesecake ice cream.

"Why is there someone following me?"

"What?" She seems genuinely shocked. But not worried.

"You know, tall guy, white suit, bad manners."

"A tail?"

Victor freezes, taking in the sincerity on her face. He turns to see people sitting alone, not eating. He catches someone staring at him, her ear pricked up like a kid eavesdropping on her parents. The woman quickly turns away, her sharp nose pointing at a cold untouched chocolate soup that used to be ice cream.

"Victor," Marilyn is still looking at him, "Is someone tailing us?"

Victor smiles, "No, just thinking out loud." He pretends to look at his watch. "You know what, I think our client's waiting." He holds out his hand for her. She hesitates and the suspicion inexplicably catches him like a needle prick.

They make their way into a sort of lobby where tons of guests have gathered.

Marilyn taps him on the elbow, "He's there. Adam Larousse."

They walk over to where Mr. Larousse is introducing two guests to each other. Larousse is a short but thin man in his thirties with an air tainted with reputation and mystery. His eyes are constantly squinted and his brown hair is tousled and long.

Victor extends his hand. Mr. Larousse meets his eyes, shakes his hand.

"Mr. Larousse? Victor Wolff, it's a pleasure to meet you."

The suspicion hangs like static on his handshake. "I'm not sure if I agree with you yet, Mr. Wolff."

"Oh, I hope I can change your mind, sir. I'd hate to get kicked out of a party."

Larousse allows himself a slight laugh, "Try getting kicked off a cruise." He looks over at Marilyn, who doesn't hesitate.

"Marilyn Finch, sir."

"A pleasure," He says, gently taking her hand, "Have you eaten yet?"

"I haven't had the chance, but I hear your chefs are a sight to see." She answers.

"Only the best." Larousse leads them to the restaurant in the corner, *The Sands*. It's a huge restaurant with fish tanks in the center, with billiard and poker tables lined up neatly around them.

"You two gamble?" Larousse asks as they wait for the food.

"Only when I'm feeling lucky." Victor smiles.

Marilyn interrupts, "Mr. Larousse, we come on behalf of—"

"And how are you feeling now?"

Victor puts a hand on Marilyn's arm to stop her before she repeats herself and throws a few tokens on the table, "Like I'm betting too low."

Marilyn glares at him and takes a deck of cards from the dish, "I'll deal."

She deals out the first round. Victor picks up his cards unfazed.

Marilyn slaps another card on the table. Victor throws two more tokens on the table.

"Bold, Mr. Wolff, I hope you know what you're playing at."

"No risk, no fun." Victor replies as Marilyn puts down her tokens.

"If fun means bled dry." Larousse raises the stakes.

Victor matches and raises further. "Tell me, Mr. Larousse, how much of this money you're betting is actually yours?"

Larousse hesitates. His tokens rattle in his hand. "What do you mean?"

Marilyn turns to Victor, shooting a warning glance at him.

"Well, a classy man on a yacht can only throw so many parties on a fixed income, isn't that right, Miss Finch?"

She mouths something Victor doesn't quite catch, but she turns to Larousse, "I never count wrong, Mr. Larousse. How is it you've managed to stay afloat?"

Larousse's eyes dart from his cards back to Victor and Marilyn. "You two kids are crossing a very fine line."

"'Thou shalt not steal' seems like a pretty thick line, doesn't it?" Victor quips.

"Steal? What have I stolen?"

"There goes 'Thou shalt not lie'."

"You're Adolf's goons?"

"Not goons, consultants, and right now, we're your last ticket out."

"What are you talking about?" A bead of sweat trickles down the side of Larousse's eyebrow.

Here it is, Victor thinks. "You've got two doors, Mr. Larousse. Behind one—"

"You don't know who you're working for, boy."

The words feel like hands pressing at Victor's throat. "What?"

"I bet you she does." Larousse says pointing to Marilyn.

"What do you mean?" She asks.

"You mean you don't know?" Larousse's voice turns to laughter, "Oh, that'd be fantastic bedtime story, why don't you ask your dad to tell you that one."

Victor can see Marilyn's jaw tighten.

The feeling of vertigo comes back in bursts, all charging at him like a running of the bulls. He steals a look around the restaurant. The same people from the ice cream shop. And the same from *The White Rose.*

Victor regains his posture, speaks calmly.

"I'm sure we'd all love to hear it, but you didn't let me finish."

Larousse frowns.

"You have two doors, Mr. Larousse. Behind one, you can find out who I work for and we do things the hard way, and we all lose just a little more than a lot of money. Or…" Victor's fingers tremble, all of a sudden he feels a cold sweat. His pulse quickens and a lump swells in his throat. He feels sick, like he's just slipped and he's staring into the black emptiness of a choice. "Or," He lowers his voice to a whisper, only Mr. Larousse can hear, "Or, you can help me get her out of here."

Larousse's expression shifts completely.

"There are spies tailing me since I got on the ship, I need to get away from them. I need to get her away from them."

"What?"

"Those are the terms. It's your choice."

He sees Marilyn straining to hear. He can only hope she didn't hear anything. But she definitely sees Larousse's face. His confused and scared expression.

"Not much of a choice." Larousse scratches the back of his neck. "What is this?"

"You said I don't know my employer…" Victor checks his volume.

"No one really does."

"I'm going to find out." The words were barely audible even at a whisper. They sounded more like a strangled breath trying to escape. Victor looks back at Marilyn. A warmth runs through him. He can't help thinking he's just plummeted down an endless pit with no way back.

"Very well, Mr. Wolff," Larousse says out loud, "You have a deal." And setting his cards face down, "Your call."

Victor smiles grimly, setting down his own cards, pushing his tokens, "All-in."

4

The ship vibrates lightly as it drifts through the stars. A jazz band dressed in red velvet tuxedos and vibrant neckties step on stage and begin breaking out a bluesy tune, melodiously matched to their eccentric suits. People stand and mob the dance floor. Victor watches from the sidelines with Marilyn, neither of them joining in the dance. He stares blankly at the musicians, his focus turned inward. Marilyn breaks his train of thought.

"What did you tell him?" She asks.

"What?"

"We didn't agree to this, you could've gotten us in trouble."

"I missed the part where we agreed on anything."

"We *agreed* that I'm here to do things the right way."

"The right way? This way works, I just saved the guy from whatever Mr. Wren's way is."

"Mr. Wren agrees with me that your way isn't ethical, that's why I'm here."

"Oh, does he?"

She scoffs away the question. "Did you get the shares?"

The muscles in his shoulder tense, his fingers twitch. "I made a deal."

"What deal?" Marilyn whisper-screams. She raises her

eyebrows, looking at him wide-eyed. A disbelief marks her dilated pupils, and suspicion darkens her expression. "What did you say to him?"

Victor turns to avoid her gaze. The musicians dish out a new series of instruments. The riffs of a smooth electric guitar growl through the speakers, sending a bluesy new wave of vibrations through the floor. The drums join in, brushing lightly against the snare and hi-hat. As if to save him from the question, the ship drowns out the music. Dancers let go of their partners to keep their balance. The musicians ignore the commotion and play like it's their last song before they die. The saxophonist's face turns purple from the effort of blowing through the brass. The drummer's arms flail playing lightning fast fills, switching out the gentle brushes for good old-fashioned wooden drumsticks.

Victor crouches to keep his footing. The ship shakes more violently than during takeoff.

Armed men in suits run their heavy-set bodies to the other side of the ship. Marilyn glances at Victor, confused. He tries to reach out and explain, but the engine noise is too loud to hear anything. Even the music is nothing but a muffle now. Instead, he grabs her hand and leads her down the promenade. He can hear her voice, but can't make out the words. He pushes people aside to let them through, not taking time to feel bad when they fall. The music! It causes a chaos like nothing he's ever seen. The muffled notes mixed with the sound of the engine amplify the stress.

A man jabs his elbow into Victor's side in an attempt to keep steady. Victor swallows the pain and suppresses the urge to punch back, keeps walking. He feels Marilyn's hand slip out of his grip. He turns to see her being dragged away by the man with whiskers. Victor rushes back to help, but Marilyn had already broken away from the man's grip and shoved him to the floor.

Wolff reaches for her hand, but she pushes him back. "Who was that! What's happening?"

"Listen, we have to get off this ship." He yells over the noise.

"Clearly!"

"That's not what I mean, I—" A hand falls on his shoulder.

Larousse's squinting eyes look into Victor's, "You have a few minutes to get down before this crowd does. The music should keep them out of it a while, now go!"

"Why are you helping us?"Marilyn yells.

"Ask your boy here, he knows better than I do. Go!"

Victor doesn't wait, he's already running toward the door. He hears footsteps behind him and sees someone running after them. One of Wren's spies. Victor leads Marilyn across the bridge. A guard slips behind them from a restaurant, pinning the spy. Victor keeps running and doesn't stop until he reaches the corner. A gunshot pierces the air and silences the music. Wolff hears a scream as soon as the report dies down.

Marilyn covers her ears, "Where are we going?"

But Victor rushes into the nearest restaurant. It's completely deserted. The smell of grilled meat is still flowing fresh from the kitchen.

"What are you doing?" She asks.

Victor pulls her into the shadow of one of the tables.

"Victor, what's going on?"

"Stay here." He whispers. It's the first time he's seen any type of fear on her face. She nods.

Wolff walks back out of the restaurant, fully expecting to see an army of spies surrounding the place, but no one shows up. Running back to the bridge, he crouches instinctively. Larousse's guard lies outstretched on the floor, a red stain blotting his shirt. Victor leans over the body, checks his pulse. Nothing. He lets out a sigh.

Another shot rings out. Victor looks back toward the promenade. Guards and spies are locked in each other's arms, pistols flying for a clear shot. The gun! Victor slides his gun out of his pocket. On his feet, he spins looking for an exit. A huge door on the floor beneath him with a window in the middle letting out onto the raging water below.

We haven't landed yet! A surge of pain spreads into his chest just thinking of the jump it would take to get down there.

"Hey!"

Victor turns to see a spy dashing at him full speed, a trickle of blood running down his forehead.

Before Victor can react, the man is on him, pinning him to the ground. Wolff finds a pistol with a silencer staring him down. "We're not supposed to kill you." The man says with a strongly accented voice, "But maybe a bullet in your leg will make you easier to—Ah!"

Victor snaps a punch into his cheek so sudden, the man doesn't even have time to flinch. It's just enough to make the spy lose balance. Wolff kicks him off and stumbles to his feet. His feet skid as he turns back for Marilyn, but the spy blocks the way.

"Good arm." His hand is outstretched, finger on the trigger.

Victor raises his hands slowly, "I get around."

"You look tired. You should come with us, we'll get you cleaned up."

"Sounds good. Raincheck?"

"No raincheck. Mr. Wren wants you back now." The gun is

almost touching Victor's chest.

"Mr. Wren will have to catch me first." He slams the gun away, grabs the spy's shoulders and jams his knee into the stomach.

The spy falls to his knee and Victor jumps around him, making for the restaurant.

"Come on, we gotta go." He doesn't even care to whisper anymore.

"Go where!" Marilyn barks.

"Marilyn, we don't have a lot of time."

She sneers, but stands up.

Leading her by the hand, Victor peeks over the side of the entrance. Three spies block the elevators and two more block the stairs, all of them with weapons drawn.

Victor lets out a sigh.

"What's wrong?" Marilyn whispers, letting go of his hand.

Victor pinches the bridge of his nose. His head hurts from the thought of three bullets to the chest. "How far down would you say the next floor is?"

"What?"

"Nevermind. You might wanna take off those heels."

The velvet curtain tears off its hooks with an effort. Victor ties it to a post at the entrance of the restaurant. He does the same with another one and hands the loose end to Marilyn. "Get ready to run."

Marilyn's face is a portrait of confusion itself, and she stares at Victor, waiting for him to explain. "You're not gonna—"

"It's either this or a stomach full of bullets."

Victor peeks over the edge. The spies are still waiting. Their guns are lowered and they're walking toward the restaurant. Victor waits a few seconds, listening to the steps, timing the jump. "Now!"

The spies bark out a series of cries and orders, raising their guns to shoot the runners. Victor jumps over the banister with Marilyn falling closely behind. The curtain grazes his skin as gunshots fill the air above him. Vertigo crawls through him, gnawing at his insides. The falling finally stops with the curtains pulling taut, their feet still a couple yards above the ground. Glass showers down on him, and the spies are already aiming over the banisters like hawks waiting to dive at their prey. Marilyn is already running for the exit. Victor takes off after her, instinctively shielding his head from the bullets as if it would help.

The door growls open and the bridge is already open for them. Right on cue, bullets begin raining down around them. Almost sliding, they hustle down the ramp onto the dock, shoving past the parade of onlookers. Marilyn slows down.

"Keep running, they'll be down soon, we have to hide!" Victor yells.

The streets of Egeria are a stark contrast to the ship's promenade. There are shops and restaurants, but all of them outside and closed up with linen sheets surrounding them. Small palm trees grown in large pots made from clay. Tiny motorized scooters are parked on the sides of narrow roads.

Up ahead, Wolff spots an abandoned little white concrete hut hiding in a corner of the narrow street.

"Go, that way!"

He breaks the dusty window and steps aside for Marilyn to go through. Victor climbs in after her.

The hut is dark and smells like old wood and spice. The air coming in through the broken window has a dry chill that makes Victor shiver. He leans his head on the cold concrete, takes a second look around to stay his paranoia.

Marilyn is laying her head back on the wall trying to regain her breath. Victor can only hope they were fast enough to lose the spies. They won't have given up yet, the best thing for it would best to wait them out and move further into the city when the coast is clear. Hopefully they wouldn't look in the hut with the broken window. Hopefully.

The moon comes streaking through the hole in the wall, gleaming off of Victor's pocketed pistol.

"Where'd you get that?" Marilyn is looking at him, pointing at the gun. He'd almost forgotten she was there. Almost.

"Boy, you really have a question for everything, don't you?" He had meant it as a joke, but it didn't come out that way. "Sorry. The guard who stopped to protect us had it on him." Lying about it makes his gut churn, but it wouldn't be the first time he's lied.

"You took it from him?"

"Trust me, I don't think he minds."

"Was he—"

"Yeah."

Her eyes fall to the ground hearing it, even if neither of them dare say it. A sadness darkens her face, but it turns into suspicion. "Why did he help us?"

The question catches Victor by surprise. "What?"

"Why did he help us? You said you made a deal with Larousse. Why wouldn't he just let them kill us?"

"I don't know. Just a good guy I guess."

"If he's bad enough to steal and then lie about it, what problem would he have with letting his problems just fade away?"

"I don't know."

"You seem like you *do* know." Her voice shakes with an angry fear, "Who were those people?"

"I don't know."

"Really, Victor! People you don't know don't try to shoot you!"

He doesn't even try to answer, just stands up and walks toward the door, clicking open the latch.

"Where are you going?" Marilyn snaps.

"To think." He answers without turning. And he walks out the door, leaving Marilyn in the dark of the lonely hut.

Victor buries his face in his hands, wiping away the exhaustion and adrenaline. He's sitting outside the hut on the doorstep, taking his chances with the spies. A groan escapes him, turning into a furious growl. Something inside him hurts. The suspicion in Marilyn's eyes. Somehow he feels he's already messing up. For a second, he wishes he was back in his apartment, forgetting all about the day. What bliss, wasn't it? Feeling guilty for a moment most nights, drowning it in a playlist of blues music, going to sleep and forgetting all about it to rinse and repeat the next day. The phrase "ignorance is bliss" comes to mind. He wishes for ignorance now. But knowing. Knowing is a curse. Knowing has him in a terrible grip, and it won't let him go until he does something about it. He knows he can't go back. No matter what he tells himself, he can't go back.

And that's why he said it. *I'll bring her back.* Because now he knows what happens if he doesn't. And it's a thought you can't drown out with blues music. He turns to look back at the hut, as if it's going to whisper some encouragement. But reality strikes him like a whip. He *did* get her back. Halfway at least. Away from Wren. It takes some of the self-pity away, just enough to look around for a pay phone.

He hurries around the streets looking both ways for spies before crossing, and keeping an imaginary rope tied from the hut to his waist. He sees a pay phone up ahead. But it means letting go of the rope. Wolff hesitates, but finally decides to go for it. He goes around the shop to where the phone is. He can't see the hut from here, but this shouldn't take long.

Victor reaches into his pocket and draws out a card. There's a name and a number typed onto it in default font. Victor clicks the number in on the dial and puts the phone to his ear.

"Mr. Crow?"

"*I'll transfer you.*" The receptionist answers.

A click sounds on the receiver. "*Who speaks?*"

"Mr. Crow. It's Victor Wolff."

Crow's tone sounds suddenly urgent. "*Victor? Is everything alright?*"

"Your daughter's safe. She's with me."

Victor notices the exhaustion in his own voice for the first time, the words drag on his tongue and there's no witty quips left in him.

"*Where are you?*"

"Egeria. Had a bit of a rough landing, we can probably get onto a Nav outta here tomorrow."

"*Perfect, bring her to me. I'll meet you in Luminoir, you'll get your reward. 10:30, Luminoir Standard Time.*"

"Yes, sir." The thought of a reward brings a pang of guilt to Victor's stomach. He feels like he's delivering Marilyn like a package.

"*Victor,*" He says before Wolff can hang up, "*Does she trust you?*"

Victor turns in the direction of the hut, knowing full well their makeshift hiding place might be found if he takes too long. "We'll see."

"*Keep her safe.*"

Victor hangs up the phone with "Yes, sir" still echoing on the line.

Something about the whole thing feels wrong. Victor takes a breath of the cold air before walking back. He feels like he's deciding someone else's fate behind their back. He dreads the moment she asks, which he knows will be as soon as he walks into the hut.

Victor's footsteps echo in the empty streets, chalk-white pebbles crackling under his feet. Apart from the dust, the streets are remarkably clean. But there's no way of losing the dust sand in from the desert behind the city. Victor always found it ironic that the city is stuck between sand and water. Desert and sea.

A cold wind breathes frost into Victor's bones making his shoulders tense up. He doesn't like feeling tense. It slows him down. His eyes rise from the floor to the hut, still a few feet away. A light flashes from the inside, sending a white beam shining out the window. Victor stops in his tracks. His hand automatically goes to his gun. At the same time, the light shuts off with a low click.

Victor draws the pistol and creeps toward the house, calculating each step. The handgun feels a little too heavy, but he keeps it balanced with both hands, cradling it into aim.

Every step makes him wince. His shadow darkens the doorstep. And he turns the handle slowly, poising himself to burst in and start shooting. But something holds his hand still, he draws his hand back, but it's too late, and the door pulls him in making him trip over the step and fall flat on his face.

A chorus of low-pitched laughing breaks out in the room before it's deadly silent again. Victor looks up slowly to see Marilyn mumbling something at him behind a gag. Her hands and feet are tied and she's looking at him behind fearful blue eyes.

And an olive-skinned man with a thick but short black beard crouches in front of him, blocking Marilyn from his sight. The man smiles.

"Ah, you must be the spy, uh," he says, "We've been expecting you."

5

Victor lets out a groan between struggling breaths. The fall had knocked all the air out of him.

The bearded man barks out a laugh that sends spittle flying. He steps aside and drops a hand on one of his colleagues to steady himself. Victor grunts again, wiping the dust off his jacket. Any thought he may have had of escape doesn't work if you're shot dead by smugglers or whatever these guys are. He wipes his mental chalkboard. Five men with cloth masks wrapped around their heads and mouths tower over him. They're staring at him behind the slit in their masks, letting only their sandy eyes surrounded by dark skin show. The one without a mask taps Victor with his foot the way you'd kick a dead animal.

"My name is Orlan Hal," he says between heavy breaths, "These are my brothers. Take one step and my brothers will slit your throats, uh?"

Victor sits up. The men train their rifles on him as soon as he moves, "Those aren't knives." He pricks, lifting his hands.

Orlan shoves a punch into Victor's stomach that almost makes him puke. The hot taste of stomach acid makes him retch. "You mock us, spy?"

Orlan's sleeve rises over a tattoo, a black scorpion.

And Marilyn tries saying something, but it's muffled by her gag.

Victor shrinks back, hugging his stomach. Between groans he answers. "Orlan, wasn't it? This looks like the beginning of a beautiful friendship."

A snarling smile touches the tips of Orlan's mouth. "That's a shame."

Wolff scoots back to scan over the men. Apart from their rifles, a curved dagger hangs from a strap on each of their chests, with a couple extra mags clipped onto their belts. He makes to stand up. The men all yell out their threats, it's amusing.

"Who are you?" He asks them.

"We're here on behalf of Emperor Priev the Third." Orlan answers cautiously.

"And what does Emperor Priev the Third want with us?"

"You'd like to know, uh?"

"Are you always this much of a pain, Orlan?"

"We're taking you to the Emperor as soon as gates open... spy." He shoots out a ball of saliva on the floor.

"Well, you can tell your emperor we're just passing through."

Orlan takes a step forward. Then another until he's staring straight down at Victor's eyes. He can smell the garlic in Orlan's breath as he speaks. "The Emperor waits for no man."

Victor smirks. "First time for everything."

Another punch hurls into Victor's stomach. He falls back on his rear. Orlan points at the other men. "Don't let them out of your sight. If he says anything, shoot his limbs. You're not going to kill him until I give the order. We need him alive. For now."

"What are you gonna do with us?" Victor asks, looking back

at Marilyn sitting in a quiet anger. She looks ready to punch whoever happens to be nearby. That's probably why they tied her down in the first place. He's not sure he'd untie her even if he could. He doesn't think he can take absorb another punch without throwing up.

Orlan doesn't even acknowledge Victor anymore. He talks to his Brothers while wrapping a linen sheet into a makeshift pillow, "We sleep here for what's left of the night, then we take them to the Emperor in the morning."

Victor slides down beside Marilyn. His hands and feet are tied now, but they didn't gag him. He leans over to whisper.

"You talk too much."

She turns to shoot a cold glare at him, which he chooses to ignore.

"Apparently my brothers here find me amusing." He waves at one of the men. "By the way, what was it you were saying about people you don't know *not* trying to kill you?"

"Quiet!" One of the Brothers comes round to kick him in the shin. A warm burst of adrenaline rushes through him, but it runs back out through the rope tied around his hands.

He makes an effort to talk lower.

"You okay?" Victor can't even tell himself if he's being sincere. He hopes he sounds sincere.

Marilyn looks at him and shakes her head grimly.

Fair enough.

Victor settles down quietly, his hands curling into fists, leaning his head against the wall. *Never let them see your fear*, he reminds himself, taking one last look at the Brothers. They're switching around once in a while, taking short shifts so each one gets a little bit of sleep. Orlan is the only one who apparently gets a full ride. Victor growls inwardly, closes his eyes. Eventually, he falls asleep.

He wakes up to Orlan's lulling, gentle kick which runs through his leg like he slept on a pile of ants and they're all biting down at the same time.

"Wake up, spies. Time to go." The sweet sound of Orlan's heavy, dusty, intermittent voice breaks down the walls of his sleep. Then, he walks out, leaving his brothers keeping watch.

Victor slowly opens his eyes, shields them from the heavy burst of sunlight beaming through the broken window. He blinks off the burning from the brightness until his eyes finally adjust. He turns to see Marilyn already standing, the gag removed from her mouth so she can breathe. But, she doesn't talk. One of the Brothers is holding a rifle to her back.

The door flies open and Orlan comes prancing in with a devious smile gleaming as bright as the sunlight. He signals to his brothers to move out. One of them jerks Victor to his feet, sending a flow of boiling blood to his head. The room spins for a moment as black and purple splotches blot out his sight. Victor covers his eyes, letting his body shake off the sleep gradually. The blotches clear as the Brother pushes him out the door, only to have to squint against the sun's penetrating glare. Immediately he feels a gust of hot air blow into his face. It takes about thirty seconds for tiny beads of sweat to form at his temples and starts streaming down his neck.

Through semi-closed eyelids he sees the day-life of Egeria flourishing at full shopping spree. He notices him and Marilyn are the only ones that look like melted wax figures. "What time is it?" He asks no one in particular.

Orlan answers, seemingly in a good mood. "Six thirty.

5

What's wrong, uh? Still sleepy?"

"What are so many people doing up so early?" Even squinting he can see hundreds upon hundreds of people rushing by the markets with baskets or bags full of early morning snacks and produce.

"This is peak hour. The sun gets too high up not much later. Dangerous." Orlan's eyes darken as he says it.

Victor has to resist the urge to look up. He doesn't want to end up a blind wax figure. One of the Brothers pushes the barrel of his gun between Victor's shoulder blades, pushing him into the bustle of shoppers. Orlan leads the way. The only way Victor can tell him apart is by the red cloth hanging on his belt. The streets are saturated with people stopping occasionally to buy fruits or dates. The exchange between seller and buyer takes place without seconds to spare. No needless talk. Just business. The heat from the crowd makes Victor sweat through his shirt. He wishes more than anything that he could take off his jacket, his arms are starting to itch from being drenched in sweat.

The guards don't seem affected by the heat, though. They must've grown accustomed to it all. This is just another day for them. Meanwhile, the heat purges Victor's limbs and his eyes refuse to adjust to the light. The crowd just seems like a bunch of colored dots floating across a white-tan landscape, with the occasional green of the occasional plant. He can half-see Marilyn walking beside him, still quiet, staring at the floor. A sadness passes through him, but the heat boils it away before he can really feel it.

Finally, his eyes acquire some sort of clarity, and he can see their destination in the distance. A huge palace with circular roofs, painted like a marble masterpiece. It looms against the sun. Victor takes advantage of the shade to take a good look around. The city's larger than Victor had imagined, and definitely more populated. Great walls surround it on every side except the sea.

The sea. He can see it through a small alley. Not even an alley, a crack. A crack between two little seafood huts. And he can see a little shrimp boat hovering on the water.

He looks back at the palace. It's not far. If he's gonna make a run for it, he's gotta go now. He looks over at Marilyn. She must see it too. He tries to nod at her, but she doesn't see him.

Victor clenches his fists. He can already feel the bullet tearing through his spine.

And the moment he makes himself trip feels like flying with a clipped wing. And the Brother falls behind him.

Victor jumps to his feet and breaks into a run for the sea. He can only hope Marilyn will follow. But he can't look back. The heat feels like it's crushing him, but his legs won't stop now.

He hears the Brothers running after him, but they've already proved they won't shoot him, haven't they?

Still, it's not enough. One of the Brothers catches up to him and shoves him down. And now he sees her. Marilyn *was* running after him. But Orlan has her pinned.

Orlan nods to his colleague. The Brother snaps a punch which leaves Victor's ears ringing. He can feel the warmth of blood in his gum.

And he can see Orlan's arm pulling back, his eyes trained on Marilyn.

And what's next is all a blur. And he feels his fist connect, rope and all. And he sees Orlan on the floor growling like a rabid dog.

"That's enough!" He barks. "You try that again, and I'll kill you myself, regardless of what the Emperor wants!"

Then he looks at his brothers and the veins in his forehead pop. He takes the one who had been guarding Victor by the collar and pins him to the wall. Orlan slides his knife out of its sheath and makes a small cut beneath his brother's eye. Even behind the mask, Victor can tell he's shaking. Orlan's eyes are bloodshot and his breath heavier than ever.

He grabs the edge of the Brother's mask and unwraps it gently. "You're not my brother. You're nothing. Get out of my sight!"

The Brother straightens and walks into the crowd. And he disappears.

Half an hour of walking through hellish heat brings the salt out of you like blood from an open vein. But the palace breathes a breath of fresh air even from its gates.

Victor feels the dehydration like black smoke filling his lungs, running down his throat, and broiling his tongue. He can hardly feel the bruise forming on his cheek, or his red raw knuckles.

But he sees the bruises forming on Orlan's face. He doesn't know how he feels about it.

A guard dressed like a Brother mans the gate, he nods to Orlan.

"Brother," Orlan says, "We have a gift for the Emperor. Let us through, uh, and he might reward you, too."

"As you say, brother," The guard answers, "The Emperor must have his spies."

He steps aside to a table where the men leave their weapons. They have many more than Victor thought, hidden in their pockets and boots, and the folds of their clothing. He can't help but feel respect at Orlan's restraint. Respect and fear. Victor watches as Orlan lays Wren's pistol on the table. His hands almost reach for it.

Orlan leads them down a large hall decorated with portraits and landscape paintings, some of which Victor recognizes from bids he's attended on Wren's behalf.

The air inside the palace makes paradise seem like an oven. It's not that much cooler, but it's air. Potted palm trees blossom along the great hall.

Two brothers open the tall doors to reveal an enormous room with a golden throne and two tall windows on the sides, opening onto a vast sea of sand. A man sits on the throne, decorated in a robe with golden jewelry encrusted on it. He lifts a finger with a golden ring on it. He's muscular and well built, but his face has a distinct roundness to it which makes him look older. He really can't be any older than fifty.

He takes a good look at Victor and Marilyn as they cross the entrance. The emperor raises an eyebrow.

"Who are these foreigners, Orlan?" His voice is higher than Victor had expected.

"My lord, these are the spies you have charged me to find." Orlan's tone had suddenly changed from the snarling authority to a servant in complete submission.

And the emperor changes from suspicion to complacency like he's switching on a lamp. "Well done, Orlan. Step forward, my spies."

Victor takes a step forward, but Marilyn has to be pushed before she obeys.

"You come into my city, and for what? So you can force me into surrendering my government to your warheads!"

Victor takes a step back, shocked. Warheads brought down governments and galactic powers over half a century ago, they taught it in history books like a legend. "Your highness, with all due respect, I don't have a clue what you're talking about."

"Don't you? Then why are you here? And running?"

"I already tried to explain to your goons here, we're not spies, we're just passing through."

"Would a spy not try to convince us of the same?"

"I'm sure he would, but.. Will you let go of me?" He turns to Orlan. Priev nods. Orlan snaps the cords. Victor rubs his wrists, they're raw from the scratchy rope, and re-buttons his sleeves, straightening out his suit. One of his hands automatically goes to his pocket. "I'm sure he would, but would he offer you something in return for letting us go?"

"Such as?"

"Your highness, what's the most valuable substance in the universe?"

The emperor thinks a while, like he's putting together a puzzle. "Power."

"A man with power such as yourself can stop a war."

"There is no war. Yet. But if you *are* a spy, you know there is one just around the corner."

"War is always just around the corner. A petty theft, a cross word is all it takes to push it over the brink. Tell me, Emperor Priev, a spy can only offer you war, I can offer you peace."

"How?"

"I can find the spy for you."

"So can my sons."

"Not like I can."

For a second, he expects the emperor to flare up and yell at his guards to execute him for mockery, but instead his face remains unreadable. "I must speak to my council. And you will join me."

"Deal." Victor stretches out his hand. Orlan jumps as if he'd put a gun to the emperor's head.

The emperor scoffs. "You're not free. I merely wish to discuss what to do with you." He stares coldly at Victor. "Orlan. Arrange the meeting, and get our spies something to eat."

Orlan cuts Marilyn's bonds and leads them to a room with a long stone table covered all over by delicious foods of all colors. The freshest fruits paired with the juiciest meats. Marilyn sits down and starts eating without so much as a word to Victor. It doesn't bother him, though, he's too hungry to care. All he wants is to eat and prepare his argument for the council. His talk with the emperor had been pure run-of-the-mouth, but now he has to figure out how he can catch the spy. Orlan shoves a cup of water down in front of him.

"You will sit here and wait until the council enters." Then he points at Marilyn, "You come with me."

"Where are we going?" She demands.

"Emperor's orders."

Victor stands up, an impulse taking over his body. "She stays. I need her to talk to the council."

Orlan lets out his dog-bark laugh. "It's not up to you. None of this is."

He walks out, Marilyn follows close behind, holding her head high and proud.

An hour later, four men appear, followed by the emperor. They take their places around the table, all of them tanned golden, and wearing enough jewelry to dress an elephant. Their necklaces fire gleams of light all over the room.

Victor shakes off the last of a nap from where he's sitting, and watches everyone sit around him.

The emperor doesn't waste any time on introductions. "As

all of you know, our world is threatened by an unknown power seeking to destroy us."

His eyes are grim and red.

"We have few clues as to who these people are or what they want from us. What we do know is that they have warheads backing them, ready to deploy their war on our planet, and we are dangerously outnumbered. We have received reports that other planets are facing the same demon. But we cannot spare any troops for them if we can barely defend ourselves."

"What about the planets that aren't threatened? Won't they help?" Victor sits up.

Priev looks straight at him, already annoyed, "Until we know who these people are, we cannot risk exposing ourselves. Until we know who our true enemies are, everyone is an enemy."

The words echo in the room, a dark voice repeating "enemy" like arrows flying toward Victor.

"If we surrender?" One of the council members offers morbidly.

"Then our planet is no longer ours, Franz."

Franz's eyes turn toward the floor, crestfallen.

"Fortunately we have one piece of information to help us. We know our enemies have sent a spy. They are watching us, making sure we are trapped."

The members all turn to glare at Victor, who can't help but shrink under their sandy stares.

"This boy, Victor Wolff, claims he is not the spy, but that he can help us catch whoever is. The floor is yours, boy."

Victor stands, and begins to walk around the room. The beams of light shine on his face. "You folks have one way of figuring out who's doing this to you. Catch the spy. And you folks only have one way of catching the spy. Me."

"And why should we trust you?" Another council member asks, a large, round man of about sixty-odd years old.

"I have resources you can't imagine. I'm a consultant. I've met people on my job, I know just about everybody who would want to start a war with Egeria."

The emperor smiles, "I'm well aware of your job, Mr. Wolff. And that is exactly why I don't trust you. I wouldn't trust Adolf Wren with any business of mine, and I certainly wouldn't trust him with warheads."

"Adolf Wren is a warlord in his own head." Franz spits out.

"I don't work for Wren. Not anymore."

The emperor's eyebrow raises.

"That's why I'm here. That's why I'm passing through. It's why I'm running. And it's why Marilyn and I haven't called him to make you let us go." Victor sucks the air out of the room. This wasn't in the plan.

The light rays almost seem to make sound in the stillness.

Finally, Franz speaks. "How can you be sure you can catch the spy?"

"Mr. Franz, you have two doors. Behind one is a galactic war in which you're already about as dead as a doorknob. Behind the other one is me, your last hope at catching the spy."

"What do you propose?" The emperor asks.

Victor smiles. It's the question he's been waiting for. "If there is a spy, he must be really happy right now. That is, *if* he can't hear us right now."

"What are you implying?" The round council member asks, his eyes squinting and his face turning red.

"I'm implying all of you are just as much suspects as I am."

Disdain rings out like a gong across the room. The emperor silences them.

"You think one of us would sabotage our own home?"

"I've seen people do worse for less. So yes, your highness, *at least* one of you...is a snitch."

And everyone is looking around the room, focusing real hard, as if they'll know just by looking at them. They'll know the spy.

"Don't worry, your highness," Victor interrupts before they stare holes in each other's eyes, "I'll find your spy. But I need to get out of here. Not that I haven't enjoyed this, but I have a prior arrangement, and I have a greater chance of finding said spy from out there than I do in here."

The emperor smiles, "It looks like we have two doors, my friends. Trust this boy and risk losing our spy, or keep him here, and risk losing our spy."

Victor hides a gulp.

"Very well," The emperor stands, "Mr. Wolff, arrangements shall be made, and you shall leave today. Thank you, my friends."

One by one the councilors walk out, leaving Victor alone with the emperor.

Emperor Priev walks over to the side of the room and opens two large doors. Victor follows him onto a balcony overlooking a huge courtyard with date palms growing along its edges, putting on a beautiful display of dancing shades. The balcony is like magic. Wind courses through the veins of the palace, and somehow the heat never penetrates its walls.

Walls. Victor sees the ones that surround the city.

"What are those walls for?"

The emperor seems serene. His face is turned up at the sun. He takes a breath in and answers, "What are any walls for? To keep people out, and to keep people in."

The words sound threatening, but he says it in such a way

that they almost soothe Victor's curiosity.

"Why?"

"Those walls are our safety, they only open once a day for two hours, enough time for a few people to leave and a few to come in."

"Like a prison."

"Like a shelter." Such passion in a phrase. The emperor must believe it fondly. "Without those walls, armies of spies could flood in uncontrolled, and we would never know until it's too late."

"But the cruise ships?"

"All authorized. Unfortunately, I was outvoted. The other councilors believe the tourism would benefit our economy. But it is controlled, by our wall. No individual could make it through without us knowing."

Victor squints to look at the gleaming water. Crashing waves roar around the port. He sees for the first time buoys floating as far as the eye can see.

"Those are sensors?"

"That is a fence. No sneaking in through there."

A faint blue light blinks on and off with the sun. A holofence.

"You will leave at the Parting Hour, when the walls open."

Victor nods.

"I don't trust you, Mr. Wolff. I have been wrong before, but I don't trust you. Or anyone who has worked with Wren."

"I'll find the spy."

The emperor turns to look Victor full in the face, with all the serenity peeling off him like a mask. "Then, until you do, the girl must stay here."

The words shake Victor. A sharp vertigo hits his stomach like an anchor, pulling him down. It makes him dizzy. He puts a hand on the banister to keep him steady. "What are you talking about?"

"As collateral. I need to be sure, you understand."

"No, you don't understand, I can't leave here without her."

"Then you will miss your prior engagement, I am afraid."

Victor hesitates. He has to think fast, but he can't be stuck here. "No, I'll go. Just don't...Don't hurt her."

"You have my word. Orlan!" He calls, but the man doesn't appear. One of the Brothers comes into the room. "Where's Orlan?"

"He is still tending to the girl, your highness."

"Very well. Take Mr. Wolff to her to say his goodbyes. Then, take him to his quarters where he shall remain until the Parting Hour. Orlan will handle him after that."

"Yes, my lord." The Brother makes for the door, and Victor has no choice but to follow.

6

The guard leads Victor through a long, narrow hall at the end of a stairway. They pass several curtained rooms drowning out the light in an attempt to ward off the heat. All of them are empty. The silence is a weird mix of reassuring and unsettling. As they go farther up it's as if they're getting farther from the sun. It gets cooler. And darker. Victor has to squint through the shadow to make out the shape of the guard. They stop at a door, impossible to describe in the gloom. The door handle squeaks. A cascade of bright white light floods the corridor, blinding, burning. Victor shades his eyes with his hand. He hears a chair scrape back.

The guard steps aside, out of the light, and disappears into a corner of the room for Victor to pass.

"Victor?"

He can hardly see through the light. Can almost feel his pupils dilating.

"Victor, are we leaving?"

"Nice to see you, too, Marilyn."

"Victor, are they letting us go?"

Victor hesitates, his eyes adjust just enough for him to see her eyes. "No. No, they're not letting us go."

Now he can see her more clearly. She's changed from her

dress to an Egerian linen shirt and pants with leather sandals. And her hair is tied up. "What do they want with us?"

Victor steps around her to the window. A small opening without bars, more of a room than a cell. But it locks from the outside, doesn't it?

The window looks down onto a desert. They have to be on the highest floor. The only thing upwards is the sky. *We should have been up there by now*, he thinks, watching the clouds slug across the blue plain.

"What do they want with us?"

"You heard them, they think we're the spies." Victor says, still looking out the window. He brings himself back in, his face shaded by the backlight of the sun against the darkness of the hall. "They want me to find their spy. But they want to keep you as collateral."

Her face changes from anger to concern, "What? What if you don't?"

"No, I can find the spy, but I have to get you out of here."

"They won't let you. They'll think you're running away."

"Yeah. I just need some time to think. They're letting me out when the walls open."

"What am I supposed to do til then?"

"I don't know."

"Just go back to Urbis, talk to Mr. Wren, he'll—"

"No, we can't go back to Wren."

"What? Why?"

"Look, you just have to trust me."

"Trust you? I'm supposed to trust you? You have people chasing you everywhere, trying to kill you! Because of you, I have been shot at, kidnapped, and gagged! And I still don't know why! How am I supposed to trust you? Who are you?"

"I'm the guy trying to save both our lives, but I can't do that if you don't trust me, so please, give me a few more days, and then you can go wherever you want, but let's just get off this planet." He knows it must bother her that he isn't raising his voice, but he doesn't even know if he can anymore.

Marilyn crosses her arms, but she nods.

"Mr. Wolff, time to go." The guard calls in. "You have a call."

Victor looks up at the guard. "A call?"

"In your room."

He nods, and leans in as he passes Marilyn. "I'll handle it, just trust me."

The door locks behind him as he steps out. The guard leads him into one of the dark rooms across from Marilyn's. Victor walks in.

"For the record, Mr. Wolff," The guard says. His eyes squint behind his mask, "You won't find the spy." And he shuts the door. The lock turns. The guard's footsteps fade away. Victor checks the door handle. Locked. He's a prisoner. But it's not a cell. It's a room. He takes a breath and turns to take in the space.

The curtain waves in the artificial wind from whatever invisible weather shield the palace has around it. The sunlight fights to get through, but only a beam manages to blink in through a corner, shining a ray of light onto a bed with white linen sheets. And a chair in the corner. He tries to lift the curtain, but it's bolted to the ground. Through the slit between the curtain and the window, he sees the city, and it's closed walls in the distance. Victor sighs and settles down on the chair.

Then a little red phone on a shelf rings. It rings like it could bring the walls crashing down like a modern Jericho. Victor lets it ring itself out. But it rings again. He has a call. And it calls him toward the phone until he finds himself picking it up and putting it to his ear. And it whispers.

"*Where are you?*"

He doesn't answer.

"*What happened, I heard there was trouble on the ship?*"

"We're alright." He whispers back into the phone.

"*Are you still in Egeria?*"

He doesn't answer.

"*Victor? Your suit dusty yet?*"

And there's a long silence. A long, death rattle of a silence.

"*Victor, what are you doing?*"

Victor can't answer.

"*You better know what you're doing, kid, because if you don't, it'll break my heart to have to kill you, Victor.*" And it sounds like regret. Like loss and pain. And a sigh, "*If this is your fall from grace, make sure you land on your feet. Or it'll break your back.*"

Victor holds in a sigh. He feels his chest burning and freezing over all at once.

"*Goodbye, Victor.*"

And the voice is gone. And the room is back to silence. To airless. To sunless.

Victor sits back in the chair, staring at the red phone, watching its big red smile. He clenches his fists.

The sun slides down the edge of the curtain. The beam of light narrows to nothing but an echo. Victor watches the city through the window slit. The sun lines up perfectly with the stone horizon of the wall. The door opens with a click behind him. A guard stands at the door wrapped completely in shawls except for his eyes.

"The wall's not open yet." Victor says curtly.

But the guard doesn't reply.

"Are we leaving?"

The guard draws a knife from a sheath at his waist. Victor steps back, gritting his teeth.

And the man lunges at him, jerking his knife. Victor covers his face and blocks the jab. The knife comes within an inch of his eye before Victor shoves it away. It flies across the room and under the bed. The guard snarls, shoving his fists. Victor dodges and makes for the door. The Brother wraps his arms around Wolff and slams him onto the wall. The blow knocks the air out of Victor.

The guard walks away and reaches for the knife, coming back to hold it up over Victor's head. The knife springs down. Victor manages to catch it with the phone, feeling the pressure on his arms. The brother's sleeve rises, and there's a black scorpion tattoo on his arm. Victor pushes the hand away, and drives the phone into the side of the guard's skull.

He falls, groaning. Victor fights through the rush of blood coming to his head to find the door. He leans on the wall, panting for air.

The guard slashes through the curtain and jumps out the window.

Victor tries to catch his breath. His eyes are blurry from the adrenaline.

Before he can reach the stairs, two guards block the way.

"The wall isn't open yet, Mr. Wolff." Says one.

"I don't care, I need to talk to Priev."

"He's unavailable at the moment."

"He'll have time for me."

"Sir, Emperor Priev is unavailable at the moment."

"So make him available. Tell him I have information on the spy."

The guards look at each other questioningly. Suspiciously.

"Come with us."

They lead him to the emperor's room. Priev's eyes turn up at him sadly. Loads of papers are spread out in front of him, showering the table with their inky symbols in the native language. A small thin vizier with a pointed nose and weasel-like whiskers looks over every sheet with careful beady eyes.

"Mr. Wolff, I assure you, we will alert you when the doors are open."

"Look you might be buying flowers, but I'm not ready for a funeral yet, your Highness, especially not mine."

"What are you talking about?"

"I'm talking about one of your guards trying to shove a knife in my eye!"

"I swear on my life, I would not send one of my guards to kill you. What would the point be?"

"That's what I'm asking myself." Victor shoves past the two guards to raise himself in front of the throne. He stares into the emperor's blue eyes. Whispering, "If you're not trying to kill me someone is."

"I wouldn't."

"Then who would? Who could possibly want me dead so urgently?"

"I don't—"

"Your Highness, I give you your spy."

"Who?"

"Who? Your very own top dog, that's who."

"Orlan?"

Victor nods. He looks over his shoulder at Orlan's brothers. "Impossible!"

"Apparently not." Victor steps back down while the emperor tries to hide his outrage. His fear.

"You two find Orlan, bring him back here. Lock Mr. Wolff in with Miss Finch."

"What? No, I found your spy, we had a deal!" The emperor's eyes glaze over with cold indifference. An Urbis taxi driver couldn't have looked more disinterested.

"If it's you they want dead, perhaps it is best that you stay."

The guards wrap around Victor's arms and hold him back. Victor strains his arms, pulling after the emperor. But the guards are strong. He feels himself fall from the struggle. His hair falls over his face and an angry sweat starts sliding down his side. Victor puts a hand to his head, where a throbbing pain begins to spread.

Blood. Not sweat.

Blood.

His eyes blur, and he barely sees Emperor Priev pointing toward the exit. And his feet dragging on the marble floor. And the darkness closing in.

Victor grits his teeth. He fights the blur to look up at Emperor Priev. At the glazed eyes of an empire at war. No mercy for the ones in the crossfire.

The guards drag him all the way to Marilyn's cell. She stands up, clenching her hands and watches the guards as they shut the door and lock it.

When they're gone, she whispers, "What happened?"

Victor can hardly talk. He tries shaking off the laziness, but sleep wants to drag him down. "You have a towel?"

Marilyn squats down to his level and checks the top of his head. "What did you do?"

"Is it that bad?" Victor groans.

She gets up and comes back from the bathroom with a towel. She helps him up and to the bathroom. Inside, Marilyn pulls on a string and a little half-dead light bulb starts swinging its pale blue light, hanging from a string.

Victor closes the door behind her as she leaves and sees the red stain on his face from the blood in the small round mirror hanging from the wall over the sink. The blood drew lines on his cheek and blots on his shirt collar. He sees where the blow landed. It's not gushing anymore, but it hurts when he even thinks about it.

He takes a breath and winces at the touch of the towel to his head. The wound stings, and all his thoughts are too crowded by the pain. He throws the towel into the sink and turns on the water, watches it rush onto the towel and turn red. A deep dark red. He can see his own fear in the mirror. Can see his pain. He licks his dry lips and holds his head, trying to think how he's going to get out of here. But there's always the pain.

And then there's a rumble on his hands, and the water shakes. The light bulb starts swinging its light in circles. He hears something like the growl of a thousand cars exploding all at once.

Victor throws the door open. Marilyn is staring out the window.

"It's happening." She says.

And for a minute he thinks she means the warheads are landing. And a knot forms in his throat. But what he sees out the window takes a grip on his gut. In the distance, the walls are sliding open.

Victor starts pacing the room.

"What are you doing?" Marilyn is looking back at him almost angrily.

"Looking for a way out." He replies, sliding his hand along the windowsill. The curtain is missing a hook. It drapes over the window, sending rays of light scattering throughout the room. One of them shines across Marilyn's eyes. And she's holding something up.

Marilyn holds up the missing hook. A trail of long white sheets streams down from it like a white veil. Victor smiles, speechless for once.

She runs past him to the window. The roof isn't far up, but there's not much places for the hook to grip onto. Marilyn swings the sheets. The orange light from the sunset creates white shadows as it pushes through them. The hook shoots up, clawing at the wall, but falls back down. Marilyn barely dodges it. She tries again. This time the hook wraps around a flagpole. She pulls the sheets a few time. The sheets tense and hold. She nods back at Victor.

Marilyn jumps on the windowsill and pulls down on the sheets one more time. "Just making sure." She laughs shakily. Victor follows her onto the sill and helps her up. She pulls herself onto the wall and starts climbing. When she makes it up, Victor grabs onto the sheets, wraps them around his hand. He takes a breath and steadies himself just as the door flies open.

A guard rushes in with his rifle drawn and aimed at the windowsill. Before he pulls the trigger, Victor jumps out of the way and sees the bullet fly into the pink-orange sky. He swings back like a pendulum and crashes into the wall. The impact shudders through his body and a pang of hot pain floods to his head. He feels the breeze of another bullet fly behind his back. Victor reaches and hoists himself up.

The guard's footsteps echo through the hall as they fade away.

"Hurry," Victor calls to Marilyn, "They'll be back."

"We have a problem." She says, and before she can explain, he reaches the top.

He looks past her shoes and sees the roof, extended through-out the palace in a slope. A steep slope. There's only a thin beam, about a foot wide through the middle of the roof. A guard calls out from behind him, already climbing the roof. They climb up from all sides.

Victor whispers. "Run."

Marilyn starts rushing across the roof like a skilled tightrope walker. Victor runs after her, trying his best to keep his balance. A bullet grazes the air near his arm, almost knocking him off balance. Wolff steadies himself and keeps running without looking back. A guard climbs up in front of him. Marilyn stops to wait.

"Just go! Run for the wall!" He yells. Hesitantly, she turns around and keeps running.

The guard aims his rifle, but Victor pounces at him and the shot bursts into the sky. The report booms through the air. The guard lets go of the gun to regain his balance, but Victor snaps a punch into his jaw and pushes him to the side. The guard tumbles down the roof and catches hold of the edge just before he falls. Victor's arms flail and he crouches to hold the beam. He fights the breeze rushing at him and stands back up, barely able to run.

Bullets fly past him until he finally reaches the end of the roof. He sees a ledge beneath him and the guards closing in on him. And he jumps. The fall sends a rush of pain like electricity surging from his feet into his legs. But he shakes it off and climbs down to the next one, grateful for the first ledge's protection from any fire coming from the roof.

The city opens up beneath him in a rush of fast trading and quick shopping while the "cooler" air lasts. Victor drops himself from the last ledge into the sea of people. And the crowd swallows him up.

He falls on his feet and stays crouched. The suffocating heat of the city washes away any trace of the air conditioning. Hoping the guards don't have an eye for finding needles in haystacks, he brushes through the crowd, looking for Marilyn. He wants to scream out her name, but he knows he'd just give himself away. So he walks, turning at every corner, but always heading toward the wall. The door.

Within minutes he's sweating like steak in a grill. His lungs struggle to find air. They burn. His head wound feels singed and shoots pain within pain through Victor's body. And his eyes strain to make out any faces among the crowd. But none of them are Marilyn. That, he's sure of.

Suddenly, the crowd freezes, and there's space between them. Because a gun goes off. A bullet fired into the air. And through the crowd, he can see the covered face of a guard. And he's staring right at him. Taking aim.

Victor runs into an alley, and he can hear people complaining and clamoring, and he knows they're getting closer. He steps into a store and walks to the vendor. "Please, you need to hide me."

The man says something in a foreign language, and makes signs with his hands.

"No, hide. I—NEED—TO—HIDE."

But he can tell it's not getting through. Victor groans, and turns around. He hears the rumble of a motorcycle and a buyer walks in.

Victor hears the cries of the guards nearby. He scolds himself and runs back out, jumping on the bike. He turns on the ignition and hears the owner yelling after him. But he can't understand it. The motor revs and the guards run up to him. Victor tears down the road, leaving a a trail of smoke behind him. The guards choke on the smoke for a second, but most of them recover quickly and are already running after him again.

People jump out of the way of the motorcycle, probably cursing at him for almost running them over.

And slowly, the guards shrink into small dots in the distance. Cautiously, Victor slows down into a plaza full of people. A familiar loud groaning roars through the air. The sound of stone against stone shakes the world around him. *The wall,* Victor thinks. In the distance, the wall is slowly sliding shut. The crack between its "doors" gets narrower by the second. Victor charges the engine again and breezes by the shops. The hot air forms tears in his eyes and boils them. They evaporate before they even touch his cheek. Guards rush in from the edges of the square. Victor looks back at them, willing the wall to stay open a few minutes longer.

He turns back to the road. And he's heading dead on toward a fruit cart. Victor jerks the bike's handlebars, but the momen-tum gets the best of him. And he feels the splintering of wood cracking around him as he crashes into the fruit cart, shattering it to pieces. Victor flies through the air and tumbles onto the ground in the midst of a cloud of black smoke, the bike skidding over him. The sound of screeching metal and a circle of smoke building up around him sounds like a robotic monster growling at him. He covers his head to protect it as the motorcycle spins to a stop beside him, almost jamming its tire into his head. His wound splits open from hitting the ground and he feels the blood begin to ooze out again.

The guards don't stop. They charge at him at full speed, guns raised. Victor coughs and stumbles to his feet, trying to run the rest of the way with a slight limp.

The opening of the wall is right there. Just open enough to let him through. He hurries, but the wall is faster than he thought. A bullet lands in the ground beside him. A warning. He turns back to see the guards. And Orlan steps from between them. Not bound, not gagged, not even hurt. He aims his gun straight at Victor's head. And he smiles.

And he puts his gun away.

Victor doesn't hesitate. Doesn't stop to ask why.

He runs as fast as he can for the wall. Growling, he bolts into the crack. Halfway through, he has to turn on his side to get through. The stone pushes onto his chest. It could crush him like dirt between its fingers. But he takes a breath of burning hot air and pushes through. And the crack spits him out in the other side.

The sun falls with him. And the planet is plunged into darkness. He catches a final sight of Orlan and the guards, before the wall slams shut, its stony growl echoing. And he sees the betrayal of an army against their emperor. And he can't imagine why.

Victor sits up and takes a couple breaths before a hand on his shoulder startles him. He turns to see Marilyn helping him up.

"Thanks." He says.

"Don't mention it." She replies, looking back at the closed

wall.

"Let's just...get on a Nav and get off this planet."

Marilyn nods.

And they walk. Away from the wall. Away from the emperor and his traitors. And away from Egeria. To the Spaceport.

7

Silence.

In the space of a few days, Victor had forgotten what it felt like to have complete silence. He had forgotten the sound of his own calm breathing. He had forgotten what it felt like to rise and fall with the movement of space. And silence.

No gunshots, no fighting, just the light brushing sound of the Nav's engines flying them toward the end of the line. Marilyn would finally be safe and Victor would be a fugitive from Wren. And worse, he would be unemployed.

The Nav's lights flicker on and off with a bit of turbulence.

Victor gets up and takes a look around. It's been a long time since he's boarded a public AstroNav. The Nav System is one of the few companies in the galaxy that Wren doesn't own... Yet.

Victor rests his forehead on the window. He can imagine the long silver tube held by spinning metal rings floating through the deep black canvas of space, slicing through the silent wasteland of stars and planets.

If this is silence, then out there is something else. It's more than silence. It's a void.

And the planets. The havens in the desert. So many astral explorers have given their lives to discover the ones where humans can breathe fresh air and drink clean water. Victor always thought those deaths were unnecessary. There are better ways of finding out something is dangerous than taking off your helmet and breathing in the poison.

He takes a last look around the cabin. Every first-class passenger had been given one of these cabins for their personal comfort during the long voyage at slightly less than the speed of light. And Victor remembers now why he had stopped traveling by Nav.

His room is a dizzying kind of white and grey of alternating shades when the blinding electric light is on. But even with the light off, the room is about as bright as a star for someone trying to go to sleep.

Victor scoffs to himself and taps one of the buttons on the panel beside the door. The white light fades to a dimmer violet, and Victor can imagine the painters putting up floodlights and painting them purple.

He groans and throws off his jacket, not caring to hang it up in the closet beside his bed. He falls back on the bed and and the slight rocking of the Nav sailing through the cosmos lulls him to sleep.

And his eyelids open at the loud scraping of wood. A pair of eyes stare down at him, wrinkling at the corners with an upturned grin.

"Are you here, Victor?" The grin enunciates.

But Victor can't find the words. A fear chokes him when he looks into those dark aquiline eyes.

Mr. Wren recedes. He leans on his table, still looking at Victor.

Wolff takes stock of the wooden furnishings around him, and the foggy window behind Wren. The room is neither bright nor dark, but both and all at once.

Wren taps on the desk, his ring scraping against the wood. Victor sits up in his chair.

"What is this?" He asks.

"Hmm? You must have zoned out, I hope I wasn't boring you." His voice echoes throughout the room, and it sounds distant, as if he's standing much farther away than he looks.

"No, sir, you weren't boring me." His lips form the words on their own. Something inside is doing the talking for him.

"Are you alright, Victor? Shall I continue with the lesson?"

"Never better, Mr. Wren. Go on."

Mr. Wren nods slightly. "As I was saying," He pushes himself off the desk and begins walking around Victor. "Loyalty, Victor, it's one of the few virtues a man is allowed to have in a business such as this."

Victor's eyes shift around the room. He feels like a puppet on a cardboard set. It's the perfect replica of Mr. Wren's office, but something's different. Something ominous. Wren keeps talking.

"A man can be loyal to one master, kid, if he becomes loyal to a second, he's a traitor to the first, you understand?"

"Yes, sir." The words slug out. He can feel his heart in his throat pulling at the strings to quicken his breath.

"So, Victor," And he stops walking when he comes in front of Victor again. He pauses and turns to look directly into Victor's fearful eyes. Half of his face is obscured by a phantom light shining on the opposite side. "Answer me this..."

Victor looks past Wren. A crack spreads through the window like a spider web. Fog rushes in and devours the edge of the room. It growls like a wild beast as the walls vanish into its mist. It surrounds him, taunting to come closer. It inches up to Victor's feet. And Wren doesn't seem to notice. There's an angry grief in his eyes. A rageful sadness.

"Why did you betray me, Victor? Who are you loyal to now?" The fog steams up Wren's body, and Victor can hardly move. He feels strings on his arms, tying him to the chair. "You can't hide from me, kid" Wren sighs as he straightens and disappears into the fog, "I'm coming for both of you."

The fog roars and swallows Victor up, strings and all, leaving everything in darkness.

And Victor wakes up.

He bolts upright, gasping. The light is a yellow blinking like a sun. A steady beeping fills the little room. Victor takes his coat and rushes out the corridor to the row of open windows. The luminescence of the lively city, awake at all hours, shines in the distance. The Nav slows to the ground, hovering low over the Spaceport. Passengers rush into a large bus-like container. The elevator.

Victor pushes past a crowd in the elevator. And he sees Marilyn dressed in a new set of jeans, a t-shirt, and a light black jacket, rid of the dust of Egeria. Mostly.

"We're here," She tells Victor.

"Where'd you get the clothes?"

She looks him up and down. "Spaceport gift shop."

Together, they walk into the box. The base clicks and a red light washes over them. A panel in the upper corner blinks out the number of passengers. Victor remembers the vertigo he felt in his stomach as a child the first times he rode a Nav. But he doesn't feel that now, the memory is all he has left of that distinct feeling. The elevator slides onto a platform, grazing the sides as it latches in. The doors slide open and the passengers rush out as urgently as they rushed in, flooding out like a burst dam. Everyone's in a rush to get home, get away from home, or get off this planet as quickly as possible.

"Where are we going now?" Marilyn asks.

"To find somewhere to sleep." And he feels a tightening in his stomach. "And something to eat."

"Why here?"

"You want to keep traveling?"

Marilyn shakes her head and starts walking into the city. Luminoir is one of the newer planets in the galaxy, but it's one of the most developed. *Coloniers* saw it as a blank canvas, waiting for a painter to brush their strokes of color and light into a masterpiece. The *coloniers* were idealists. And French. Still, it'd be a lie to call it anything but a masterpiece. Now, it's the planet of artists, chefs, and fame. All famous actors, musicians, and, ironically, painters live in Luminoir. It's like an obsession in their interviews, it comes up at least once in every sentence.

The city's flooded with bright blue light with screens at every corner advertising all sorts of products from creams and lotions to cars and clothes by the most famous designers. Fancy restaurants and huge mall shops beam forth invitingly at every corner in gaudy propaganda posters and famous spokespeople.

Night is deep into its shine, the moons at their peak, and not a soul in this place is asleep. Every store stays open, every restaurant still serving late-night meals and midnight snacks and breakfast for dinner for the off-clock brunchers. It's a city of night owls running around under the weight of their heavy shopping bags, even heavier from the humid air.

The clouds begin to sprinkle shiny droplets into the streets. Somehow it makes the city even more beautiful. The fountain in the middle of the plaza stops spitting out water. Shoppers run to "find shelter" in stores.

Victor and Marilyn slip into a restaurant at the corner of a street named *Rue Lavalle*. The place is packed with people hiding from the rain like cockroaches from the light. There's nowhere to sit except the bar. Victor pulls out a stool for Marilyn and sits down beside her, turning to face the door. A poshly dressed bartender walks up to them, an empty glass in one hand and a cloth in the other. His sleepy eyes scan over Victor. In spite of the weariness, there's a sort of owl-like keenness in them.

"ID?" He asks, raising his voice over the commotion. Somehow, the patrons are whispering and yelling at the same time.

Victor passes him a card. The bartender stares at it for a moment, like he's reading between the lines of an essay.

"You're nineteen?"

"And a half." Victor answers.

"And you?" He asks Marilyn.

"I'm not nineteen."

The bartender scoffs, "You can't drink."

Victor smiles back, "Can we eat?"

The Owl nods as if to say *"Try to resist."* He puts down his glass and cloth and draws a notebook and pen from his apron. "What can I get for you?"

"I'll have a Filet Mignon, medium well." Victor says.

Marilyn looks over the menu, her eyes reading every description. Finally, she says, "I'll have a Coq au Vin, please."

"Sure thing." The Owl rushes over to a large slot with sweet-smelling smoke puffing out where a small-eyed man in a toque and apron delicately decorates a dish with a juicy slab of meat. The bartender says something and the man looks over at Victor and Marilyn and smiles familiarly, the smoke bringing his attention promptly back to the food.

"You've come here before?" Marilyn asks.

"Chef was a friend of my parents. We used to eat here all the time."

"You're from Luminoir?"

"No. My parents like to travel. They like to eat."

"I'd eat anything at this point."

"Why eat anything when you can eat here?" Victor answers with a smile. A smile she returns.

And a steam blows in between their smiles as two gleaming white dishes slide in front of them. The most delicious smell of cooked meat and runny sauce waft into the air. Victor takes in the scent. He remembers his parents bringing him for the first time.

What would they think if they saw him now. Would they be proud?

He leans in and takes a bite of the pinkish meat. The juicy flavor explodes in his mouth and he closes his eyes to enjoy it. When he opens them, he sees Marilyn doing the same, and for a second, he forgets they're the ones escaping. And he laughs.

There's nothing left on either dish now. Marilyn puts down her fork. She stares at her plate, deep in thought.

"What? Still hungry?"

"What are we going to tell Mr. Wren?"

Victor freezes. He realizes he's still keeping up his little farce. And he can't give it up now, "Marilyn, we can't go back to Wren."

"What?" Her eyes turn to him, "No, I mean, we'll explain why we couldn't get the share. Those people were trying to kill us, Victor, Mr. Wren will understand."

"Wren won't understand." He feels the sting of the bend in the truth.

Marilyn lets out a breath. "Why?"

It's a question he can't answer.

"Why won't he understand, Victor?" But again, she's left talking to herself. "Fine." She pushes the chair back under the bar and walks out the door. Into the rain. Victor watches her hail a cab through the droplet-covered door. But he can't bring himself to go after her.

He sighs and buries his face in his hands. The exhaustion is finally catching up to him. He feels a pressure at his chest and groans. And the bartender comes back. "Everything alright, sir?"

Victor looks up and smirks, "Peachy." When he turns, he sees the gloved woman staring at him from across the restaurant. He recognizes her from Hunt's party. Victor flinches and begins to get up, but when he turns again, she's gone. He sits back down and asks the waiter for the check. The waiter looks down at him, watching as he signs.

He says, "I'm sorry."

Victor feels a tightness at his chest. A pressure. An instinct. And he knows what it is. He's had too much experience to not know. He feels the gun at the back of his head. And the waiter taking cash. And the restaurant is suddenly empty. And it was all a trap.

"Go to your motel." He hears the voice behind him say, "Stay there. We'll be watching."

The gun vanishes into thin air.

Victor spins around ready to blast down anyone in the way. But there's no one. He thinks of strangling the waiter, but remembers he's being watched. And he's not that guy anymore.

And he remembers Marilyn.

Victor runs out the door and hails a cab.

The motel is on the outskirts of the main city. A shabby box of rooms. The lights have faded in this part of the world, the stars nowhere to be seen. Clouds loom in the sky like boats splashing water onto the world below. In a moment, Luminoir had lost all its beauty.

Victor climbs the stairs, almost tripping over a vagabond sleeping on the steps. The vagabond grabs his leg and urges him strongly to watch where he's stomping. Then, he walks into the room. Marilyn sits on a wicker chair next to a phone and a lamp. The room is small: two twin beds, a couple of chairs, one lamp, and a main fanlight on the roof. Victor practically tip-toes over to the other chair and sits down. He feels like he's walking on the very narrow edge of a very deep pit. "Mar—"

"Who were those people?" She interrupts softly, "The ones chasing us on the cruise ship?"

"I told you—"

"You lied. Everyone seems to be chasing us. Why? Please, don't lie to me, Victor."

Victor sighs. He's never found it harder to lie. Reluctantly, the words slip out, barely a whisper. "I'm trying to keep you safe."

"Keep me safe?"

"If I'd wanted to get those shares, I could have."

And Marilyn hesitates, like she's trying to think of what to say.

"What was your deal with Larousse."

"He helped us escape."

"Escape from what?"

There's a thin beam of moonlight sliding through the window. That's where Victor's eyes are set, watching that moonbeam's weak glow.

"Victor, escape from what?"

"From Wren." Victor says. He sees the confusion in her eyes. "Marilyn, you have no idea who we're working for, do you? People disappear without a trace. They don't come back."

"Come back from where?"

"Six feet underground."

"You mean he kills them?"

Victor doesn't respond.

But she shakes her head and stares at the moonbeam, avoiding his eyes. "How do you know?" And there's something more than rage in her eyes.

He can't explain how he knows.

"I'm his secretary, he wouldn't kill me."

"People are expendable."

"What?"

"He told me that once." There's a silence, and the moonbeam disappears for a moment. "You think you're the exception?"

"Well, now he's going to kill us anyway." She says, "And you've been helping him, now all of a sudden you're trying to be a saint!" Marilyn kicks her chair back and storms out of the room.

Victor stands up, ready to run after her this time. But his feet are stuck to the ground. He sympathizes with the explorers now. The ones who take off their helmets. And he breathes in the poison.

But he sees her come back. She whispers, "Victor." The fear in her voice rings like a bell.

Victor walks past her, drawing the gun from his pocket.

A man in dirty, ripped clothes stands on the step outside the door, holding his hands out, his dirty face looking up at Victor. A crooked smile gleams behind his beard, and Victor recognizes the vagabond from the stairs. "Are you Victor Wolff?"

"Who are you?" Victor asks.

"Someone who knows someone who *really* wants to talk to someone named Victor Wolff."

"Who?" But he's afraid he already knows the answer. Or part of it at least.

"Follow me." The man starts walking down the stairs. He pulls an umbrella out of a basket and hands it to Marilyn. He has a funny gait, almost like an ape walking on two feet, unsteady and cross-footed.

They follow the man into an alley. Victor feels his gun in his pocket. He primes his hand in case he needs to reach for it and make a move fast. The vagabond opens a door on the side of a building. They climb several sets of temporary stairs until they come to the top floor. The building itself is under construction, and tubes, pipes, and beams are spread out everywhere like an x-ray of a skyscraper. The concrete floor is the most developed part of the place. The building has no walls, and the rain splatters in. Marilyn folds the umbrella before a brutal gust of wind can come in blowing like a hurricane.

A woman stands with her back turned to them, looking over the city at the thunderstorm like some sort of deranged art critic. Her hands curl around each other behind her back. Her gloved hands. Victor flinches. He steadies his nerves before walking toward her. *Never let them see your fear*, he reminds himself.

"I've seen you before. Why are you following us?" He has to raise his voice to compete with the howling wind.

She holds a hand up. "Not 'us', Mr. Wolff. Just you."

Marilyn looks accusingly at Victor. He ignores the glare.

The gloved woman keeps talking, "You can call me The Source, Mr. Wolff, and we are on a mission."

"Congratulations, feel free to leave me out of it."

The Source turns around, her green eyes almost seem to glow in the dark, like a cat's. The blue light of the city shines behind her, and her silver suit gleams with its reflection. "Our mission, Mr. Wolff, is the same as yours. To bring down Wren's empire."

Victor walks up to her. He notices guards at each corner flinch. He sees Marilyn follow. And he says, "That's not my mission."

"But isn't it?" She returns, "What is it you want then, Mr. Wolff?"

"It's not about what I want. I'm just trying to keep a promise."

The Source looks over at Marilyn, who stands determined. She turns back to Victor, "And what better way to do that than Wren's end?"

Wolff pauses. His mind runs through the details. He turns to Marilyn, then back to The Source. "Wren's end?"

She nods. And three words come form the Source's mouth. Three simple words which carry the weight of planets. "We kill Wren."

"What!" He hears Marilyn scoff.

The thought had never even occurred to Wolff, it seems like heresy, a subject you unconsciously don't even touch. He instinctively steps back. The Source smiles. Victor realizes his reaction and straightens back. He almost laughs. "Great, you kill Wren, Wren's empire crumbles down on top of you, how does that fit into your plans?"

"It won't, Wren's empire will die with him."

"That's just naive—"

Marilyn steps in, "What are you going to do, shoot him? He's not easy to get to."

"We understand the risk, and we are prepared for it. What we have planned is a lot more subtle."

"Your plan won't work."

"So you have already said, Miss Crow."

The clouds seem even darker and the winds more intense. "That's not my name!"

"No, it isn't, you have no living name. You're no one."

Marilyn almost lunges at her, Victor has to hold her back. He feels her shoulders fall back and her muscles relax.

"Men like Wren don't like the thought of dying." He says, "They put measures in place to make sure they never do, and if they do, they make sure whoever does get to them remembers it for the rest of their short lives." A blast of lightning makes the sky look like shattering glass. "Listen, Miss Source, you can't kill men like Adolf Wren."

And the smile disappears. "We'll see." The tone in her voice deepens to a grave near-whisper, "In that case, Mr. Wolff, I'll say it in a language you'll understand. You have two doors: help us..." She pushes past him and starts walking toward the stairs, "Or get out of the way."

The words are clearly final. Victor sees her disappearing down the stairs. He takes the hint, and he's left standing in the rain at the top of a half-finished building, watching the shattering glass of the sky, with his helmet off. Breathing in the poison.

8

Victor walks by Marilyn back to the motel. The night is getting old. It's wearing him out. Victor wishes the sun would come up already, he hates the length this day is taking. As if dawn would take away all the exhaustion of the day. Marilyn, for her part, doesn't look at Victor once on the way back.

The motel has an even danker smell than before, like the rain made some hideous fern sprout fungus that smells like rotten dew. It's suffocating, but Victor's too tired to notice. He collapses onto his bed and shuts his eyes. The mattress is hard, like sleeping on the floor. Except the floor is carpet. And thoughts start gushing through his head like blood from a bullet wound. It drowns out the sleep. But at least the sheets are fresh. Everything else about the motel feels old, overused and outdated. Even the clock lags behind the actual time. *The time!*

Victor sits up and picks the alarm clock off the night table, almost ripping the cable out of the socket. The clock reads 11:17, which probably means something more like around about 11:30. Victor jumps off the bed and rushes across the room. Marilyn's glare follows him. He picks up his watch and coat and throws on his shoes.

"What are you doing?" Marilyn decides to break her vow of

silent treatment.

"We have to go." He replies without looking at her.

"Go where? We can get a Nav tomorrow. Nobody followed us, I made sure."

"Yeah, well, you can never be too sure. These are Wren's people, they're practically invisible."

Marilyn stands up. "Victor, if they followed us here, they'll follow us onto any Nav we board."

"You have any other ideas?"

"We can go back to The Source, they can protect us until they pass."

"I have a better idea, you just need to trust me."

"Trust you? You've given me no reason to trust you!"

"I've gotten us this far." It's taking forever to tie his shoelaces.

"Trust you to do what?"

"If I told you, you wouldn't be trusting me." He stands up and holds the door open. "Are you coming?"

Marilyn crosses her arms. "I think by now I have a right to know."

"I think by now I have a right to travel without a tail, but here we are." Victor's voice is calm as ever, but a needle-prick tension flares through him every time he's about to speak.

Marilyn's voice rises with every sentence. "Victor, we can't keep running!"

Why is she making this so difficult? He's just trying to get her safe. "Then let's make sure this is the last time. Come on, I have someone meeting us in the square."

"Who?"

"Someone who wants us safe." He walks out the door. Marilyn follows.

"Was that so hard?"

Victor sighs as he jogs down the stairs, "You have no idea."

They walk to square, Marilyn yapping out questions, Victor half-answering them the whole way. The square is abandoned for the most part. The rain is pouring down in marbles the size of quarters. Along the way, Victor picks up an umbrella from the corner of a clothing shop. He watches people still shopping, even this late, in the rain, and sits down on a bench by a dormant fountain in the middle of the plaza. Marilyn stares down at him.

He sighs to himself, "What now?"

"Who's picking us up?"

"He's on his way, trust me, you can trust him."

'Trust. You use that word a lot."

"What's the world without trust?" Victor replies with a grin.

"Trust is a two way street. You don't trust me, why should I trust you?"

"It's gotten you this far, I must be some type of lucky."

In the distance, behind Marilyn, Victor sees a man wrapped in a fur coat. He's coming out of a quaint coffee shop, shivering and sweating even before he gets rain-soaked. An umbrella hangs ironically like a black cloud over him. His black, gelled-back hair is glimmering with droplets of rain in the blue light of the city. As he comes nearer, something changes in his blue eyes. Victor recognizes it. Fear. But it turns to relief as quickly as if it had been shot off him, and a slight, thin-lipped smile lights up his face.

Victor turns to see Marilyn already watching. The man walks toward her, hands held out to the sides. Like a hug. But her fingers curl up into fists, nails biting into her palms. Victor stands up beside her. For a second, he feels like she might draw a gun out of nowhere and shoot him. He has the vaguest instinct to hold her back, but her eyes are frozen on Norton Crow.

"Did you call him?" She seethes through her teeth without turning.

"He called me."

"Why is he here?"

"He's your out, Marilyn."

"I didn't want an out, not if it's him."

"He can protect you."

She finally turns to him and yells, "He killed her, Victor! He killed my mother!"

"Marilyn—"

A tear slides down Marilyn's cheek, mingled with the water from the rain. Somehow it sends an actual sting into Victor's stomach. Crow reaches them before Marilyn can walk away.

"My daughter, I've finally—"

"I am *not* your daughter!" She hisses.

"Please, I can explain everything. If you'll come with me, I can get us somewhere safe, and then we can talk about it. Please"

Victor watches Marilyn's face carefully. Her eye twitches slightly. Her teeth are gritted like she's biting down the pain. The fear he sees glistening in her eyes is one he knows too well. Like a rabbit looking at the wolf in its last moments. Like a prey studying its predator. It's the same look that was in Mr. Hunt's eyes before Victor left him to Wren. He imagines it's the same way he would look at Wren now.

"Please," Whispers Crow.

"Mr. Crow, if we're going, we should leave now." One of Crow's guards comes up to say.

Crow nods and turns back to Marilyn, then to Victor. "Mr. Wolff, I believe a reward is in order."

Victor cringes. Marilyn turns to him. "You *sold* me to *him*?"

"I didn't do it for the reward." It sounds like a lie, even to him.

"Don't lie! I can't believe it!"

"Marilyn," Crow interrupts, "He brought you to me so you could be safe—"

"Safe! How could I be safe with *you*?"

The smile had long vanished from Crow's face, only a deep heartache wrinkles his forehead now. "Please, Marilyn, I will explain everything."

"I don't want your explanation. I don't want your apology, I want you to stay away from me!"

"Please, Marilyn," Victor puts a hand on her shoulder, wondering if it will mean anything, "Wren will find you anywhere you go, he'll consider you a traitor. You won't be safe unless you go."

She scoffs and shakes his hand off coldly. But she stops fighting. She seems to understand, but her eyes are downcast. The guards lead her away. Victor stays behind, watching her fade away in the rain. Crow shakes his hand. His smile returns, only less genuine than before.

"Thank you, Mr. Wolff. Thank you for bringing my daughter back."

Victor just nods, the droplets falling through his hair and tracing lines on his face. The last thing he wants to hear right now is a thank you.

"If you will come with me, I have your reward in place."

"I told you, I didn't do it for the reward."

Crow nods, confused but not willing to argue. "What will you do now?"

Victor makes a vague attempt at a smile, "Find somewhere to cry myself to sleep. After breakfast I might try to find some hole I can crawl into."

"A hole?"

"Wren's not gonna forget this anytime soon."

"He owns more than half the galaxy, how are you going to escape?"

"I'll do what I always do: talk my way through it."

"There's no talking to Wren."

"No, but there's talking to others. Others who don't like Wren. I've got time, haven't I?"

"All the time in the world may not be enough."

Victor sighs.

"But," Crow continues, taking a look at the cafe, "I'll help you where I can. After I get Marilyn to safety, I can take you over to Urbis. That might be the best place to start" He takes a moment, and the smile vanishes again. "She'll tell me to leave her alone."

"Probably."

"And she'll never forgive me."

"Probably not."

"But I need to know she's safe from Wren."

"She'll be safe. Besides, Wren will be too focused on me to care."

"Let's hope."

Victor smiles grimly, "Let's hope."

"You're sure I can't give you a ride?"

"I'll find my own way, thanks."

Crow turns to look at the coffee shop again. And that look comes back to his eyes. Fear. Suddenly, he shakes Victor's hand and leans in. He whispers, "There's a man at the cafe who wants to talk to you. He's been following me since I got here a couple of hours ago."

"Who?" Victor studies the people at the coffee shop. All he sees are the usual Luminoir shoppers.

"I don't know. But I can't lose her again, Victor. Please."

"I'll take care of it, you get out of here as fast as possible."

Crow nods and thanks him, then leaves. He leaves Victor standing in the rain, his feet splashing toward the coffee shop.

A bell rings when he opens the door. He can feel the fear gripping his throat. Every move feels like it's in slow motion. He doesn't even feel himself sit down. Looking down at the face of a brother.

"Ey, Mr. Wolff." Orlan says.

And Victor feels himself come back. "Orlan."

"You drink coffee?" He raises a hand for a waiter and orders two black coffees.

"What are you doing here?"

"I'm on a mission, I'm here to save your friend."

"What are you talking about?"

"Coffee." The waiter places the two cups in front of them. Orlan opens a packet of sugar and pours it into his cup. Victor smells the bitter scent of the drink. He's never been one for coffee. And he doesn't trust Orlan.

"Save her from what?" Victor enunciates.

"Drink some, uh, it's gonna get cold."

"I'm not thirsty."

"You need coffee. To stay awake, uh?"

Victor reluctantly slurps up a gulp of coffee. It burns his tongue and thaws out his throat, but he doesn't care.

Orlan nods and smiles. He takes the cream and lets it drip into his coffee. It spreads through the blackness like blood in water. "So, you made it out of Egeria. I'm proud of you, brother."

He hates it, but he knows this game. And he knows he has no choice but to play along. "You let me go. Why?"

"Let's just say I got a change of orders."

"From who?"

"The Warheads. They wanted you dead, then they don't want you dead. What do I do? Well, I strike first, then I don't, uh?"

"Is it Wren?"

"Tell you the truth, I don't know, I just talk to the middle-man."

"What are you saving Marilyn from?"

"I like her name, it means like rebellious, or bitter, like coffee, uh?"

"Save her from what, Orlan?"

Orlan takes a sip. "Okay," He puts down the cup and leans in, "One of my more careless colleagues, he accidentally puts a bomb on Mister Crow's Nav, I don't tell him this, but my boss, he wants you alive, Wolff, uh? But I don't think he minds Miss Bitter dying. Now, I am your brother, you know this, I am trying to help you. You became my brother in Egeria, and I care for you, you... Amuse me."

"What's your point?"

"Well, it would be a shame if my colleague at the bar," he points behind his back to a man waving a small controller under the counter, almost out of sight, "Were to accidentally click that small red button, uh?"

Victor hesitates, thinking. He leans in further, "If you blow up that Nav—"

"I think you had better get on that ship, Wolff."

Victor kicks back the chair and makes for the door when Orlan cries out, "Oh, and Wolff! My colleague will make sure you get home safe, uh? We wouldn't want any accidents."

Victor catches up to Crow. He'd been waiting at a bench outside the square.

"I'm sorry, Victor, he told me to wait here or he'd shoot her." Crow practically begs.

"It's fine, I know."

"What did he want?"

"I'll take that ride now." And he sees out of the corner of his eye, the red button flashing. And Orlan's colleague smiling.

9

The engines hiss to a start. Crow's private AstroNav is about a quarter the size of a commercial one. Wolff had been in a private Nav several times before. Wren's however, was about twice this one's size and was as lavishly furnished as a Nav could get. Crow is clearly a man who favors practicality over luxury. The seats are not expensive leather, but a comfortable fabric similar to that used in military AstroNavigators. Unlike commercial AstroNavs, private Navs don't need a dock to hover over while the passengers descend. And Crow's Nav is planted in the middle of what looks like an enormous underground parking lot for rich people spaceships. The ramp lowers like a tongue sticking out of a dark mouth. A bright white light shines on top of it like a spotlight.

Victor and Crow arrive long after the others. The ship is apparently ready to take off, and the heat from the engine burns a bright blue. Marilyn glares down at them from her seat, judging every step either of them takes. Victor climbs the ramp and sits down beside her. Crow's guards are yelling something over the sound of the Nav grumbling, anxious to take off.

Victor straps himself down. Take-offs in small Navs are usually anything but smooth. He turns to Marilyn, who turns away from him and looks forward defiantly.

"Marilyn," He tries to say. The roaring of the engine drowns him out. Or she's ignoring him. "I'm sorry, alright, but it was for your own good."

He tries to believe it, but now he's not so sure. He can almost feel the pulsing of the bomb on the ship. He wonders where it might be and thinks of finding it and throwing it out, but he can feel the eyes of Orlan's colleague staring him down. He can imagine the little red button pressing down and blowing them all to shreds before they can even feel the free fall of gravity.

The corners of Marilyn's mouth flinch upward. She looks about ready to tell him off. But she holds it in, something she's burying deep inside. Victor sighs and turns back to his own thoughts, which scream at him scoldingly: *Never let them see your fear.*

But Orlan knows his fear. And he can't escape it.

Crow finishes talking to the pilot, who walks past them coldly and takes a seat in the cockpit. The door slides shut. Crow climbs up the ramp, his fur coat flying and wrapping around him with the wind from the Nav. He takes a seat in front of Victor and Marilyn, yelling out one thing as he clicks the belt in, "Don't worry. It'll all be alright soon!"

The two lights beside the ramp begin to flash red, and a siren cries out in a consistent wail. The ramp screeches a bit before sliding smoothly inwards until it finally shuts, leaving them in darkness before dim yellow electric light rods flicker on above them. A puff of steam exhales with a hiss of the airlock. Then comes another screech. A beam of light shines across Victor's face as he turns up to see where the noise is coming from. A window opens up above them, he can't tell if it's glass or some other metal, but he can tell the whole ship is a lot more fragile than it should be, Navs always are. The doors open onto a vast expanse of stars resting in the night sky, and two moons watching over them all in half smiles.

The stars, they get closer as the Nav shakily rises from the garage. Victor tries to grab on to something, his body fighting the turbulence. But his eyes are fixed on the sky. It's something he realizes he hasn't really done in a long time. He'd forgotten what it felt like to really look at the sky. It made the fear shrink to the size of one of those stars, immense but distant, a dot in the expanse.

Crow breaks the silence, "It really is something, isn't it?"

Even Marilyn is staring out the window in wonder, the million stars reflecting in her damp eyes. A tear runs down her cheek, carrying the weight of her fear. One single tear, which she immediately seems to regret letting go. She turns back down and rubs it away.

The five guards in the cabin are the only ones not looking up. They look more like soldiers, than a regular security detail. They refuse to let their gaze stray from Crow, Victor, and Marilyn, as if one of those stars might sneak their way in through a ray of light and steal their passengers away. Victor looks back at them. Their helmets are off, but different color cloths cover their mouths. Victor studies their faces. There's something in their eyes he knows all too well. Distrust. Distrust in him, Marilyn, Crow, maybe even each other.

"You gentlemen sick or are the masks a style?" He decides to prick them.

One of them laughs, a guard with a blue mask. Out of the corner of his eye, Victor sees Marilyn silently roll her eyes.

The guard who laughed answers, "They're for security pur-poses."

"And here I thought you trusted me, Norton." Wolff says with a smile.

"It's not you I don't trust." Replied Crow.

Victor looks over the guards. "If you don't trust your own entourage, is there such a thing as trust in the universe?"

The men stir.

A bad feeling swells through Victor.

"There is such a thing as money," Crow answers sullenly.

"Not always."

"No. Not always."

"Where are we going? Trust me enough to tell me that?"

"A vague farming planet on the outskirts of the system, I can't remember the name. Something with an S."

"Figure retiring there, get some cows, live the simple life? The goods."

Crow smiles. "Victor, I think we both know you're not cut out for the farming life."

Victor hates the way this conversation is dragging out. He tries something else, smiles, "I guess I just can't sit still."

"Sitting never got anyone anywhere."

"It's getting us to that farming planet, whatsitsname."

Crow nods, "I'll go find out the name." He gets up and walks over to the cockpit with the guard with a green mask following him. The door locks as soon as he steps inside.

The cabin is immediately plunged into an awkward silence. Victor takes a breath and whispers. "Marilyn, I'm sorry."

And he sees one of the guards walking over to a radio and typing something in. Then turning a button.

A static noise comes from the radio. The red-masked guard messes with the dial.

"Sorry for what?" She asks not deigning to look at him.

"I'm sorry I didn't tell you about my deal with Crow."

She scoffs, "You're not sorry for selling me out? You're not sorry for putting me exactly where I never wanted to be?"

And music starts playing from the radio.

"Marilyn, listen, your father—" Victor stops.

Because he recognizes the music.

And the red-masked guard comes back from the radio, blocking out the other two. Brown-Mask shifts beside Victor.

And the song keeps playing. And Victor knows the words.

Marilyn follows Victor's gaze before she turns her back to him.

"Don't turn around. Just sit down like you were before." He whispers urgently. She sits back down, looking at the floor.

And he's staring at the knife, being drawn from its sheath.

And the singer starts singing:

It's a life for the young,

And a thump comes from the cockpit, but the door is closed. The guard turns to look for a split second. And Victor lunges forward and takes the gun out of the red guard's holster. He flips Red-Mask onto his back into the seat beside Marilyn. As he falls out of the way, the black-masked guard cleans a knife and slides it back into the sheath at his chest in the seat in front of them.

And the music keeps playing, *It's such a rich life,*

Marilyn stifles a scream. Victor pushes his knee into Red-Mask's chest and trains his gun on him. He risks turning away. Blue-Mask lays pale on the seat, his body limp beside Black-mask, with a wound at his chest gushing red. And Brown-Mask aims his gun at Black-Mask.

Black raises his hands slowly. Victor's hands twitch on the gun, and Red-Mask laughs, "What are you going to do, Mr.

Wolff? Shoot us?"

It's a life for the crooks, the wicked, and the masks,

"Don't tempt me. Marilyn, take his knife." Victor sneers back, watching Red-Mask carefully hand his weapon over.

"We both know you won't do it."

"You don't know *me*," Brown-Mask growls.

And Black-Mask stands up, pushing Blue-Mask's body out of the way before Brown-Mask yells at him to sit back down.

"What? Who are you?"

"I *will* shoot, don't come any closer."

You won't believe,

The things I've seen,

Black-Mask steps slowly closer to Victor, ignoring Brown-Mask, his boots thudding on the metal floor echo with the beat. They avoid each other, circling the cabin so that Victor and Brown-Mask end up on Blue Mask's side, and Black-Mask by the ramp.

And a piano riff starts playing.

"This can get ugly very fast, or you can give me the gun." Black-Mask says.

Victor changes aim to Black-Mask while Marilyn holds the knife to Red's throat.

"Don't give it to him." Brown-Mask says.

Black wraps a gloved hand around Victor's gun, drawing out his knife with the other. And Victor remembers the gun in his own pocket. The one they don't know about. And he lets go.

"Sit down."

Victor silently obeys, taking a seat beside Blue's corpse.

Brown-Mask's hands shake as he holds the gun. "I said don't move!"

"And I said SIT DOWN." Black-Mask aims at Marilyn. She

lowers the knife. He hands the gun back to Red-Mask.

Victor looks out the window, the Nav begins to shake slightly. The sky is shifting from the deep black nothingness to a light blue. He takes steady breaths, waiting for the guards to settle their fight.

"I will shoot!" Brown-Mask threatens again. Black-Mask inches forward. The guard's finger flinches onto the trigger. Victor turns back to the window, the atmosphere is barely touching the ship. And Brown-Mask's finger is on the trigger, putting slight pressure on it. Brown-Mask flexes his finger.

"Don't!" Victor jumps out of his seat and tackles him to the floor. The guard struggles to get free, but Victor rips the gun out of his hands.

Black-Mask whistles, "Nice job, kid, I was beginning to think you were gonna let him di—"

Before he can laugh, Marilyn jumps up from behind to knock Black-Mask off balance. The other guard reaches to free his colleague, but Victor throws himself onto him, launching them both onto the seats.

Marilyn holds the knife to Black-Mask's neck, "Stay down, don't move."

Victor backs away with the other guard's gun. "Nice."

She takes Black-Mask's gun without answering him.

Red takes his chance and slashes through the air, slitting Victor's hand. The gun drops and Black-Mask picks it up. He slashes his knife at Brown-Mask, burying it into his chest.

"Alright," He sneers, staring down the barrel of Marilyn's handgun. The bright light of day shines through the window on the roof, "This is what's gonna happen. I'm going to kill one of you, and lose half my bonus! But I'm gonna enjoy it."

He snarls and leaps at Marilyn. But a shot rings out and he

falls halfway into his jump. Black turns and holds a hand to his side. Blood spreads through his uniform. He takes his mask off as a drop of blood trickles down the side of his lip. And Victor stands over him with his own gun aimed. "You.." Black-Mask begins to say, but his words get caught by a rattle in his throat.

And Red-Mask barrels at Victor. His knife gleams, but Victor holds his arms at bay. He kicks his foot into the guard's shin. Red falls back groaning. Victor raises the gun but hesitates. Marilyn is aiming hers at Black-Mask, who lies bleeding out.

Victor walks cautiously around Red and takes a strap from the seat. He ties himself down. Marilyn anxiously starts doing the same. And the music rises to its crescendo:

What a life,

Red-Mask rubs his shin and stands to his feet.

"Victor, what are you doing?" Marilyn asks.

"There's a guard up front, and the pilot might be one of them, too."

Red-Mask stares. His eyes wrinkle like he's smiling.

"As long as they're locked up in there, they can do whatever they want with us."

"Victor?"

He takes a final breath. And he shoots. The bullet flies past Red-Mask.

"You missed." He snarls.

But there's a whistle mixing in with the piano. Victor shoots again in the same spot. And the whistle becomes a wheeze.

And the music blares.

It's a life,

And the wall splits open, being torn to shreds by the pressure's claws. The wind roars at them.

The wall of the Nav flies open piece by piece, sucking out

seats and cargo. The dead guards' bodies fly out the wall, and Black-Mask follows them, screaming. The screeching siren blares again, and the red lights flash for a moment, but go out when a shard of metal runs through them.

Victor's ears ache from the wailing, and his chest feels like it's shriveling up every time he heaves in a breath. And Marilyn shuts her eyes tightly.

Red-Mask clasps onto Victor's leg, his nails digging into Victor's calf. Wolff kicks at him with his other foot but his grip won't falter. Little by little, the Nav begins to steady. Victor kicks with all his strength at the guard's hand. The seat groans under the weight. It bends forward, suddenly semi-dropping them. Victor's hand catches the belt, burning his palms. He lets out a yell as Red grips on tighter.

It's a life!

The Nav steadies, but it doesn't slow down. Marilyn kicks rapidly at the guard, and he finally lets go, flying into the clouds. Victor lets out a breath and hoists himself up. He straps back in, Marilyn beside him. And he closes his eyes.

The Nav crashes forward. Dirt flies into their faces, and blades of grass swarm around them like bees, stinging them. Shards of loose metal dive past them. He feels them bite at his hands and feet. And his seat screeches. It flies off its hinges, and he falls. Falls. Falls.

And the music screams out from the radio, into its grand finale:

IT'S A LIFE FOR THE KINGS!

And it's all darkness.

10

Victor coughs up a cloud of smoke. The dust particles fly in front of his face, sticking to his sweaty forehead. He can feel the soot in the air. He can taste it. Rays of sunlight bleed through the hole in the Nav. A wave of humid heat blows at him from the outside. Victor lets a groan escape him and unbuckles. He falls on his chest, blowing the air out of his lungs. He grits his teeth through the pain. Wolff spits out a clot of pasty saliva. It's got a red tint to it. He turns himself over and sees the overturned Nav. He takes in a breath which makes him cough again.

"Victor," He hears Marilyn call out to him weakly. Her hair is caked in dirt, and her face has traces of smoke splattered on it.

Victor lifts himself and climbs back up to help her. He tears a shard of metal off the wall and cuts the belts. He catches Marilyn as she falls and lets her down gently. They sit taking in the silence of the breathing wind. Even the rays of sun seem to have a sound to them, almost like peace.

"We have to go. We can't stay here." He says and brings her arm over his shoulder. She steadies herself on him. They limp to the wall ripped open by the pressure. The Nav looks like it's been torn to shreds by the talons of a giant hawk.

"Where are we?" Marilyn finally finds the strength to ask.

"I don't know." Victor answers, looking for footing to climb out of the ship.

The glass crackles beneath their feet. Victor lifts her over the edge of the hole and climbs up, using pieces of seats for footing. They slide down the side of the Nav and land in a field of tall grass. The blades brush against their elbows, extending for miles in every direction. They whip and sway back and forth rhythmically, as if they're dancing to a song.

And the song is a death march. He can hear the choir of mourners singing. And in the distance, shadowed by the sun, stands a man in a dark gray pinstripe suit, a wool coat, and a dark brown hat. Victor feels a force pulling him forward.

"Wren," Marilyn says it like it's being torn from her lungs.

Victor starts walking, almost against his will, following the pull. He notes the two bodyguards behind Wren. One of them is wearing a green mask.

Victor gulps down the knot in his throat. "What are we doing here, Wren?"

"I think you mean 'sir'. And I could ask you the same question, Victor."

Wolff takes a few more steps and realizes for the first time as the grass splits what Wren is hiding behind the blades. Clasped in his gloved hand is a small knife, brandished under the gulping neck of Norton Crow.

Victor stops in his tracks, "What are you doing, Wren?"

"No, Victor what are *you* doing running with this coward?"

"Wren, don't do this, let him go."

Marilyn lets out a cry as tears begin to stream down her cheeks. She had come to stand beside Victor.

"You know, this coward vanished after you two left, he went and hid under his rock. It took a while to find him, but I guess I should be thanking you, kid."

"This is between you and me," Victor tries, "Let him go."

"I trusted you, Victor, and you betrayed me. What am I supposed to do?"

Marilyn's eyes are fixed on Crow's face.

"You too, Miss Finch. What a shame. I never thought you'd run back to the man who killed your own mother." Wren clicks his tongue.

Marilyn doesn't answer. She's paralyzed. Only her hands curl into fists.

"I'm...disappointed," Wren goes on, "I honestly thought you two had what it takes. I was wrong. I thought I taught you better, Victor. But I never taught you to go chasing rabbits."

"You scared we'll find some? We know what you did."

"What did I do?" He smiles bitterly.

Victor turns to Marilyn. He can't bring himself to say it.

Wren smiles and swallows. "Hm, but it wasn't all me, was it, kid? Never seemed to be a problem before. What makes *her* so special?"

"Don't twist my words."

"Don't twist *your* words, Victor? You really are lost down your own rabbit hole, aren't you? You haven't been my consultant, kid, you've been my right hand." He says it looking at his right hand. The hand with the knife. The knife at Crow's throat. "But suddenly here is one death you can't live with."

"Let him go." Victor enunciates.

"Oh Victor, yet another death on your resume. Yet another splash of blood in your hands." His hand slides away, and the knife slashes. Crow's final breaths fall away to nothing. And his body falls into the tall grass, burying him beneath the dancing blades.

Marilyn yells, but it's nothing but a hollow sound. The blades dance. She runs at Wren with her fists clenched and throws a punch which sends him staggering back. The two guards step forward and grab her arms. And the blades dance. Victor slams into one of them, but the other pushes him to the ground and binds Marilyn's hands behind her back. And still, the blades sway. Wren comes himself and ties Victor up. The guards hold them and push them into his sight.

He sneers and soothes his jaw. "This didn't have to happen."

"Are you gonna kill us?" Victor growls.

"It would be a waste." And he nods at the guards.

Victor feels himself get dragged through the grass. He sees Marilyn disappear in it. He feels the sharp pebbles grind into his back. And he feels the grass dancing to his death march.

Victor breaths heavily. He doesn't know where he is. All he remembers is being here.

It feels like a dream.

But it's not. It can't be. And he sees Wren's shadowed-over eyes looking at him from under the brim of his hat.

"Why'd you do it Victor?"

But Victor doesn't feel like answering. He can't. "Did you send Orlan?"

"Is it because of her?" Wren continues, ignoring Victor's question.

The silence brings out other noises. The creak of old wood. The swinging of a tired ceiling fan. Victor looks at the door behind Wren. And the door beside the table.

"Is it you? You have the warheads?"

"Of course it is." Wren nods. "I told you not to get attached. Not to ever get attached, especially to her.

"I told you, Victor, it wouldn't happen again, I took your advice, and I listened to you when you asked me for that favor, but I warned you not to get yourself attached."

"Alright, you wanna know why I left?" Victor snaps and jumps to his feet. The chair kicks back and falls, "I left because I found out who I was really working for."

And Wren smiles viciously. "You knew who I was all along, because you and I are the same person, Victor. Don't act like you didn't know. We're just two kings. It's a world for the—"

Victor shoves the table at him, knocking it into Wren's chest. He makes for the nearest door. And the two bodyguards come rushing in.

"Don't kill him." Wren says.

And all three of them are aiming their guns. Victor takes his pistol and aims it at the guard. He shifts to Wren.

And Victor runs out the other door, still aiming.

"Let's see how far he gets." He hears Wren cry out behind him. And he's running. The grass whips his legs. And he runs, leaving behind the old wooden shed in the middle of nowhere.

The two guards are running after him. Victor drops to a crouch. He can hear the footsteps, and holds his breath. They come closer. They get louder. He pricks his head up to hear them. And he feels it, his arms twitching, letting him know how close the guard is. And he pounces. The bodyguard topples over and Victor slams a fist into his jaw, and puts the cold touch of a gun against the guards cheek.

"Where is she!" He hits him again.

The guard groans.

"Where is she?" Victor repeats. He feels his blood burning. And he feels his finger feeling its way toward the trigger.

But it all goes dark.

Dark with a rush of pain to the side of his head.

He's conscious. Barely. He feels the fall. The gliding through the air. The dirt. Marilyn over him. Asking. Concerned.

"Victor, are you okay?"

He leans up, rubbing his temple, nods. He feels the ground, laced with mossy stone and a concrete floor. His arm had broken his fall, but he groans trying to get up. Victor props himself up, and he sees the walls rising all around him. And Marilyn steps back. His legs feel like they've just been crushed.

He can see the wooden plank they lowered/dropped him on at the top of the pit, rising away from him.

Wren peeks his head over the edge. He eyes them with pity. "What a shame." He says, looking at Marilyn,
"People die mysteriously all the time. They fall down the stairs, break their necks. Or they drown in the pool on the top floor of a four-and-a-half-star hotel. No one will miss your father."

Marilyn's eyes narrow as Wren gives them a last shameful look before disappearing.

His vanishing steps sound on the soft grass. It sends a tiny shower of pebbles sliding down the wall of the pit. The hum of an AstroNav sounds in the distance not long after. The still-present footsteps of the pacing guards on the edges of the pit fill the hole with their threatening echo.

Victor stands and walks around the hole, matching the pace of the guards, moving wherever they move, taunting them only with a glare. And he measures the walls. He doesn't know why he does it, he knows it's useless. The pit is just too deep. But if he sits down, he'll have to talk. And he's too tired to talk.

The hours slug through the day. The same steps of the same guards in the same darkness of the same hole, and the same eerie noises cornering them from all sides.

This planet isn't one of the hostile ones no one has settled on, but no planet is safe from everything, and he can't imagine what's lurking in the tall grass above. He doesn't *want* to imagine it.

Eventually, Victor's legs give in and he sits across from Marilyn. Her eyes are red and puffy from hours of silent tears. The anger had drained her and drained out of her. What's left is a shell of something she was, which in a moment she gave up.

Victor sighs, leaning his head back against the dirt-wall.

"How could this happen?" She whispers, almost to herself.

Victor finds that nothing he can say would help, so he stays silent.

"Why does it hurt, Victor?" She goes on, "Why do I hate him?"

Victor picks up a blade of grass and fiddles with it, wrapping it into knots. He feels a pull in his throat, and he hates it.

"Wren just solved all my problems. So, why does it hurt?" Her fist clenches tightly.

Victor drops the knotted string of grass. "Wren *is* all your problems. He's all my problems, he's all of everyone's problems..."

He looks up at Marilyn. She's shifting restlessly.

"Marilyn, it wasn't Crow."

"What?" Her tear-stained eyes look up at him.

"Wren killed her." He can tell the words physically hurt. "He killed her, just like he's killed a thousand others. Without thinking twice about it."

Her hands tremble at her knees. "Why?" The word is shakier than the grass in the wind.

"She saw something she shouldn't have. I don't know what it is. If I did, I'm pretty sure I would be underground in a coffin. Not in a pit. That's what he does to people who get in his way."

A gleam of realization passes through her eyes. Droplets begin to stream down her face again. Her teeth grit together, the anger inside her reaches its peak. It's like watching a kettle boil. Every word she speaks shakes with fear and rage. "Why didn't you tell me?"

A scoff escapes him, and he immediately regrets it. "Would you have believed me?"

A quiet moment makes his words reverberate off the walls. The light of the sun still shines through the hole. As if that circle of light in the midday sky had been made specifically to fall on this pit, so that the hole in the ground would not be left alone, in the darkness.

"I want to break him." Marilyn mutters under her breath.

"What?"

"I want to break him, Victor, I want to find whatever it is he's hiding. We can't let him win."

"We have no choice. The only way we're getting out of here is if—"

Before he can finish the sentence, a whistle blows through the air.

The body of a guard peers over the edge. And his body tumbles onto the floor of the pit. Victor jumps on the guard to pin him down, but a trickle of blood runs down his chest. Victor checks for a pulse. Nothing.

And a thud sounds from above. After that is silence. Silence. No footsteps on grass. No pacing. Victor slides the guard's gun out of its holster and hands it to Marilyn. He cocks his own pistol and waits, watching the sky anxiously, Marilyn kneeling beside the guard, searching him for more weapons.

"Just the gun." She whispers.

"Right." He answers. He'd barely caught what she said, his attention is fixed on the edge.

A familiar voice breaks the silence.

"Well, Mr. Wolff, you seem like a hard man to kill." And the gloved woman towers over them, standing at the edge of the pit.

"I get that a lot. Luck must love me."

"The guards don't."

"Yeah, they don't like to lose. You bring a ladder by any chance?" He moves his finger slowly toward the trigger.

"As a matter of fact, I did." She smirks, a thing which gives Victor a bad feeling. "The offer still stands, Mr. Wolff. Help us kill him."

Victor turns to look at Marilyn. Her eyes are downcast and thoughtful. She turns to him and then to The Source.

"Help us get out of here!" She says.

"If you come with us."

"Is Wren really that hard to kill?" She growls. Victor can see her finger already on the trigger, hand shaking.

"Do you want to stay in that hole?"

Victor scoffs. "I told you, killing him won't do anything."

"I disagree."

"Clearly." He locks the gun. Getting into a fight from a pit won't help his case. "Look, Wren is hiding something. Something dangerous. If you kill him, we might never know what it is. It could mean something way worse than Wren."

"We have a team in place to dissolve any negotiations he may have made after he's been terminated."

"It won't work, trust me, I made those negotiations myself."

"Right now, that is not important, what's important is stopping Wren before he can do any more harm."

"You're not listening," He hates looking up at her, it makes him feels powerless, "Wren can't die. We don't stand a chance if he does. Killing him is too dangerous a risk."

"In that case, you're better off staying in that pit. Away from the fight. Goodbye, Mr. Wolff."

Victor puts two fingers to his eyebrow and mocks a salute. He sits back down. He can hear The Source leaving. For a moment, he thinks of calling out. Of agreeing to her plan. He goes over the scenario.

Hypothetically, they get out of the pit, rush over to Urbis, find Wren comfortably seated behind his desk and pull the trigger. And the chaos flows out like blood. Planets explode, war rages across the galaxy. And Wren gets whatever it is he wants from it. And then the human race comes to its tragic end.

He can't let that happen.

Wolff walks back over to Marilyn.

She glares at him, "That could have been our ticket out."

"We can't kill Wren, Marilyn." He locks his gun and puts it back in his pocket.

"I know that, but we could have gotten up there and figured it out once we're free."

"If we betrayed her, she'd have us killed, which means we'd be dead, Wren would be alive and well and king of the universe for all we know."

"They'll never be able to get to him." She says, throwing up her hands.

"It doesn't matter if they can or can't, either way Wren wins. Anyway, I don't wanna be a pawn for any of these people. They're all monsters." He says, but the sting of his thoughts sends a shiver down his spine. *We're all monsters.*

Marilyn scoffs and sits down, her voice shakes, "I'm done with monsters, Victor. All of them. And I want them to *feel* all the pain they've caused."

Victor slides down beside her. The exhaustion is finally getting to him. He hasn't slept in a while, but a while feels more like an eternity. "We can't kill him, Marilyn."

"I don't want to kill him... But I don't want anyone else to die."

"They won't."

"We have to stop him, Victor."

"We will."

"We have to stop you." But he can't tell anymore if it's her saying it or if it's just in his head.

And his eyelids start to droop. Slowly, they slide shut like blinds closing, blocking out the light, and the gun in his pocket weighs less and less.

And he falls asleep.

11

He watched from a shadow in the corner of the living room. Their faces were red and the skin under their eyes was dug into coves as they were huddled up on the sofa with the news on a screen in front of them at low volume. But it wasn't the news which made them cry. It was what Victor had come to tell them. Supposedly.

And they cried.

Victor saw her cradled in her father's arms. That was the last time.

"What are you doing here?" She whispered to him.

And he answered, "My name is Victor Wolff, I'm here on behalf of Mr. Wren."

"What can Adolf Wren do here?" Her father asked.

"He offers his deepest condolences."

But he wasn't there to offer condolences.

That's not why he came.

And her father said, "We don't need his condolences, you can leave. Tell Adolf to keep his nose out of our business."

Victor nodded. He remembered nodding because he then said, "She meant a lot to Mr. Wren as well. As a secretary."

He started to leave, but her quiet voice held him in place.

"What are we supposed to do now?"

Her red eyes held him back. The door seemed too far away to reach. But he had to leave. He hadn't come to offer condolences. Still, he was sorry for her. He could imagine the wind heaving on the roof of that building. A woman he'd known once, falling. He didn't cry because he's not one to cry, but he'd felt something when he heard the news like an internal storm. And he was sorry.

She had always been kind to him. Like a mother.

But that's not why he came. He had orders. Orders he didn't understand, but orders nonetheless, and he knows better than to ask questions.

He wishes he hadn't come. It would all have been much easier.

It didn't matter.

He had to pull the trigger. That's what Mr. Wren had said.

He hadn't come to offer condolences.

That's not why he came.

Victor watched them cry as he walked out the door.

12

Dirt?

The thought comes unconsciously from behind Victor's closed eyes. Before his mind can fold back into itself, his nose twitches with a floating speck of dust brushing it on its way down. Wearily, Victor opens his eyes, blinking away the sleep. He takes stock of his surroundings and rubs his nose. The beautiful sight of a wall in front of him makes him regret waking up.

Then he remembers.

Dirt.

Victor looks up and presses himself to pounce. A rush of adrenaline bursts through him, but he's left looking at a bright blue sky.

He sighs and sits back down, waiting for the adrenaline to cool back down to a simmer.

Marilyn is still asleep next to him. He stays looking at her for a minute. He's never seen her so peaceful. What an illusion sleep is. It's peace in your own mind while your body is caked with soil and smoke, and you're stuck in a pit.

He groans a yawn away. His lower back aches from the hard ground working as his bed.

Victor sighs deeply and stretches out his back, rolling his

shoulders. The weight in his pocket comes back. His hand coils around the form of a gun and he quickly draws it away. An accident is the last thing he needs. His legs swerve when he tries to stand, both of them are asleep, like a thousand little ants are climbing up and down his body.

Dirt.

A shower of it comes raining down on him. Victor dodges the dirtfall, brushing the soil out of his hair. Marilyn coughs herself awake. Both of them look up, shielding their eyes from the sun's gleam.

A hand comes between them and the sun for a split second, and Victor hears whispers coming from above.

"Hey!" He calls out. The whispers stop abruptly, and the wind takes over. Victor winces at the hoarseness in his voice. All at once the discomfort dawns on him. The heat suffocating him in the pit. The sweat drenching his neck and back, making his shirt stick to his spine. The sunlight singeing his eyes. He's about to call out again when Marilyn beats him to it.

"Hey! We know you're up there!"

A cold moment passes. And Victor thinks he might be hallucinating because he sees a small head peek nervously over the edge before immediately disappearing, like a turtle retracting into its shell after taking a look to make sure it hasn't been moved. The turtle whispers something and returns. This time the whole head is visible. The child stares at them with arched eyebrows and a scrunched up button of a nose.

"Hey, kid, don't be scared, it's alright." He thinks asking the kid who doesn't look strong enough to lift a hat onto his head for help isn't the most effective idea, but he's not about to let an opportunity pass him by.

Marilyn seems to get the hint. "Don't worry," She says in the most good-natured, don't-worry-we-won't-hurt-you voice he's ever heard from her, "We won't hurt you."

The kid looks over the edge again. He speaks in a voice about as small as a mouse's. "Who are you?"

Marilyn answers in the same sweet tone, "I'm Marilyn, this is Victor. What's your name?"

"Vincent." The kid completely loses whatever suspicion he may or may not have had against them. He swings his feet over the hole and sits on the edge, sandals dangling high over Victor's head. "You look dirty."

"Yeah? How do you think we *feel*?"

Vincent's eyebrow arches.

"Don't listen to him. You think you can help us, Vincent?" Marilyn brushes a piece of dirt out of her hair.

The kid can't be any more than seven years old, but he seems to get the idea. "You mean a rope?"

"A rope, a ladder, a trampoline..." Victor answers.

"I know where to get a rope!" Without hesitating, Vincent rolls back onto his feet and kicks dirt in their faces as he runs away. Coughing up dust, Victor cries out, "A sandwich wouldn't hurt either!"

He means it, he feels like he hasn't eaten in ages.

"Nice kid." He says to Marilyn.

"Yeah, now let's just hope he comes back with that rope."

"I just hope he comes back with that sandwich."

It takes a while, but Vincent finally comes back, dragging an older kid—probably around thirteen—with him. And a rope.

"Miss Marilyn, I'm back!" He yells almost loud enough to make the sky itself break. "I brought my brother!"

"Good job, Vincent!" Marilyn looks genuinely proud.

"Hey, we better hurry, yeah? I don't know if we're supposed

to be out here." The older one whispers. As if the whole planet hadn't heard his brother already.

Taking a look back, he throws the rope down, letting it unfurl until it reaches the bottom. It turns out to be about a foot longer than they actually need, but he's not complaining.

Victor tugs on it, just to make sure the teenager can lift him. The skinny kid is deceptively stronger than he looks.

"You think we can trust whoever's up there?" Marilyn whispers.

Victor gulps down a dry throat. For some reason, he's been avoiding looking her in the eyes the past few hour. Probably the guilt. But now he finds himself looking up. He clears his throat and sniffles. "I trust them more than I trust this hole. And I'd trust anyone who'll feed me at this point."

A smile appears, then fades at the corners of Marilyn's mouth. "Me too."

"We're ready!" The kids are staring at them from above, the older one looking around with impatient wariness.

Victor nods. Marilyn clasps the rope and wraps it around her waist. The kids begin to heave as she helps them by finding footing wherever she can. She's skilled, the wall is like an old friend. To him it just looks like a plain old enemy.

When she's over the edge, they throw the rope down to Victor.

The rope is scratchy and a few strands are loose here and there along the length of it, but overall it seems sturdy. He wraps the rope with the best knot he can remember.

The vertigo hits as soon as he's pulled off the ground a bit too harshly. His head spins and purple blotches form in his vision.

"You alright?" The teen whispers.

"Never better." Victor groans. The purple spots fade away. He keeps climbing. Halfway up is about fifteen feet from the ground. The rope is beginning to blister his hands, and his feet are too weak to find good footing, but he plants his foot on a thin rock sticking out.

Thoughts are blurry as they pass through his mind. He takes a breath before going on. And the rock breaks away.

Victor grips the rope tighter as he swings through space. He does his best to find something to grab onto on the wall, but his nails just claw at dirt. The vertigo is coming back, but he fights it down with a deep breath.

Then it gets worse.

A loose three strands of the rope begin to unravel the other two. "Pull me up."

The rope spins to its last strand.

"Pull me up!"

They pull harder, but the rope just begins to split faster. Victor wraps the rope around his arm and flexes his muscles to pull himself up. He hangs on to the top of the rope, praying for footing. And the split at the bottom of the rope snaps. He feels the end tap his leg, still swinging from where it was tied around his waist.

The effort drains him, but he manages to pull himself up a bit farther. The kids finish the job and pull him up the rest of the way. When he's at the edge, they grab him by the arms and lift him over. He tumbles onto his back and heaves in heavy sighs of relief. The grass is wet from the spray of some kind of automatic sprinkler. The spittle of the little machine buried underground showers on top of him. He doesn't mind it. In fact, he welcomes it as it wipes away the sweat and grime from his face and suit.

After a minute of letting him rest, the teen pulls him to his feet.

"You look terrible."

Even without a mirror, Victor imagines he must look like a restless zombie freshly dragged out of the dirt. Still, saying it out loud didn't seem necessary. "You don't look so hot yourself." In a way, it's true. The kid is wearing leather shoes without socks, brown shorts, a dirty off-white shirt and an oversized brown golfer cap.

"I definitely don't look as bad as you."

Marilyn holds herself together. Somehow, she doesn't look like she's just been pulled out of a literal hole in the ground. "You ready to go?"

"Where are we going?"

"My parents' farm is about a mile that way," Vincent points eastward. The sun is nearly setting behind them as the walk toward the farm. The teen, whose name they learned was Marcus, barely spoke, while Vincent never stopped talking.

Finally, the smell of fertilizer and the sight of corn reveal the farm, a big rust-brown building in the distance.

"You can hide here," Marcus says, "I'll be back with some food."

The farm looks more like a petting zoo. Ponies and small pigs, and small cows are grazing in the pasture. Vincent had laid out something like a couch made of hay for them to sit down on.

Marcus drags the barn doors shut, leaving only a little crack in the door for a little ray of light to squeeze its way through. His footsteps mix with Vincent's in the tall grass, splashing through the dew from the sprinklers, and the footsteps fade.

And the darkness plays its part. And the breeze plays its part. And it brings a new clarity. The foreign stimuli vanish from the mind, and the fog lifts.

"He wants me alive…" He whispers to himself.

He can hear Marilyn turn to him. "What?"

But he gets up without answering, waves away the flies trying to land on his face.

"Victor, what?"

He brushes through the hay and walks with his hands out-stretched. "Look for a phone or car keys or anything useful."

He hears her footsteps, but she's not searching. "We're not going to find any of that in here, it's a barn."

"We have to get out of here."

"Why?"

"Wren wants me alive, because he knows I'm his best bet at getting them." He pushes away a hay bale, kicking at the tools frantically.

"Getting what?"

And he stops. He turns to look at her. The thin streak of sun falls right over her eyes.

"The shares."

"The shares? You think that really matters to him anymore?"

"The shares are everything. He needs them, but he can't get them all without me…"

"What are the shares for?"

"We need to get that file."

And the clarity dies with the dark.

The barn door grinds open, gnawing its way to the wall.

Victor lifts his hands, stands in front of Marilyn.

Because there's a shotgun aimed at his chest.

"Please don't shoot."

And Marcus comes running.

"Stay back," The man with the shotgun tells the teen. "What

do you want with us?" He grumbles in a voice that sounds like a boiler heating up. He fingers his gun familiarly, like he's not gonna miss if he fires.

"We don't want trouble. We just need your help."

The man's face relaxes a bit, but his shotgun is just as stressed as it stares them in the face.

There's a long silence. Victor takes advantage of it and looks the man over, finding weak points. But it's too dark. All he sees is a red plaid flannel shirt and a hat.

"Why were my children with you?"

"They got us out of the pit." Victor points in the general direction of the hole in the ground. "They brought us here. I'm not asking you to adopt us or anything, we just want food and some supplies."

"Please." Marilyn adds the magic word.

The man lowers his gun the slightest bit and eyes them over. He scoffs when he looks at Victor. He's making assumptions, Victor knows. Assumptions can be dangerous. Others have made that mistake before.

Finally, the man nods. He steps aside to let Marilyn pass first. Victor passes him, and feels more than sees the actual size of the man. What he sees is the stubble dotted across the man's face like tiny needles.

He leads them to a quaint white cottage. A blonde woman probably in her late thirties or early forties sits on the porch, scribbling in a little black notebook. And her smile quickly fades as soon as she sees the two worn and grime-splattered tramps following her teenage son down the walkway to her home.

As they get closer, they hear a faint snipping, like scissors cutting through strips of paper.

The man nods at her and she shuffles quickly into the house.

Then he turns and blocks the stairs.

"Wait here."

He disappears through the black door.

The snipping stops.

Then the man comes back out and nods at them from the door, letting them pass. Victor thanks him and crosses the threshold into a modestly furnished room, with a couch in front of a small radio and a kitchen wafting out smells of some sort of cake or pie. The front windows let in bright streaks of sunset, bathing the house in orange light and sending specks of dust visibly floating through the air. Marcus and Vincent sit crestfallen on the stairs, but looking up at Victor and Marilyn seems to raise their spirits. More Marilyn than Victor.

"Kids, go upstairs." The man says.

And their spirits are dashed again. They stomp up the stairs. A man stands at the back of the house, putting down his shears, leaning on the wall. He seems to be in his early thirties, skinny, but muscular. And short. The grime on his face and gray on his hands freshly tainted by the garden in the yard, framed like a painting by the back window. He glares at Victor, eyes squinted. Victor is about to ask about him, but a sharp scraping interrupts his train of thought.

Flannel pulls a chair out from the white wooden table and signals for them to sit. Victor and Marilyn obey.

Then the stern glance turns to Victor, flashing a glare at the gardener first. "Who are you?"

"My name is Victor Wolff," Victor feels the gears in his mind turning again, like a muscle left idle for too long, just starting to get back in the swing, "I need you to listen very closely..."

Asserting his authority usually works when dealing with people who think they have authority, and he notices the slightest cues on the man's face that it's working now.

"We've been to the corners of the system trying to stop something that's gonna happen, and the person who's gonna make it happen. So far, it hasn't worked. But I have a plan—"

"That doesn't answer my question."

"I'm getting there. I—"

Marilyn breaks in, "Sir, the man we are trying to stop is Adolf Wren. Do you know who that is?"

Victor sighs. He notices a glint of anger—or fear?—in Flannel's eyes as he turns to look at the gardener. Wolff studies the man's expression, half-listening to the conversation. The face is blurry out of the corner of his eyes, but his hands shift from his work-jean pockets to his jacket pockets.

"I know him." Flannel answers.

"Well, that man—"

"That man," The hunger doesn't matter anymore. The exhaustion doesn't matter anymore. Only the gardener matters now. And getting out of here as quickly as possible. "That man has hired me to let you now he is going to buy your farm from the Traders. And he is doubling your wages in exchange for double-time production. We tried to stop him, but he won't listen to reason."

Then it happened. Exactly what Wolff had expected to happen. The gardener's hand twitches through his jacket. Where he must have a gun hidden. A quick look of confusion flashes across his face.

"And you need my help?"

"We need you to decline his offer."

Marilyn is staring at him, asking questions with her eyes.

"And why would I do that?"

"Because the Traders offer one benefit Wren doesn't."

The gardener shifts his weight.

"Which is?"

What's he getting ready for?

"Security. As soon as you accept, Wren will send dozens of teams to make sure you're doing the job right, not to mention speeding up production. How can you expect to have security for you and your family, when you have a bunch of strangers hanging around your house." He says it looking directly at the gardener at the back of the room.

Which is a deadly mistake.

The gardener leaps across the table, shoving Flannel aside and knocking Victor off his chair. Wolff's first reaction is to flail, aiming a kick at his attacker's stomach, but he's too close for Victor to get a good hit. The gardener pins Victor's shoulder to the floor with his right hand and presses a heavy elbow over Wolff's neck, choking the life out of him. He takes his other hand out of his pocket. Victor braces for the blood. And he feels a prick in the arm. The gardener is pushing a long, thin needle with a capsule full of a yellow-green liquid into his arm. A syringe. The needle digs into Victor's skin, straight into the vein. Wolff throws a punch into the man's love handle, sending him tumbling off. Victor has to take a deep breath before getting up. He turns to see Flannel aiming his shotgun, trying to get a good shot at the gardener, but Victor's in the way. The syringe hadn't gotten its venom fully out, but it's about half-way full now. Half-way empty.

The gardener recovers and flies at Victor again. Wolff blocks a punch aimed right at his jaw and manages to nail one into the gardener's stomach. He sees Flannel taking aim. But he's not aiming at the gardener. Work-Jean stumbles back, but he rebounds, barreling all his body weight into Victor. Wolff crashes into Flannel. The shotgun fires into the roof, and Flannel trips over a loose board. Marilyn immediately drops down, scrambling for the gun. Victor finds his balance and raises his fists again, primed for the next attack.

Then he remembers it, feels the weight of it in his pocket. He notes the man's footing and counts the seconds for the right moment. The gardener starts full sprint at him.

And a split second slows down between the gardener's first and second steps.

Victor pulls the pistol from his pocket and fires a round into the gardener's shoulder.

And another bullet flies into his chest.

The gardener flies backward, dead before he even hits the floor.

And Victor's finger is on the trigger.

But he turns around, and smoke is rising from Marilyn's gun. The one she's holding out with two trembling hands, aimed at the air where Work-Jean's chest would be.

And she's shaking with fear.

13

The report from the shotgun had not been so loud. He thinks it had not been so loud. But it leaves a shrill ringing in Victor's ears. Everything seems so...distant. Dim. He can sense more than hear Marilyn asking him if he's alright. Is he alright? She seems so far away. And a gun is in her hands. Shaking. His vision blurs, and deep purple dots seem to consume everything like parasites crawling out of the wooden panels of the walls. Consuming. Melting away everything he can see. Like an old film reel burning away the picture on the screen. Keeping his balance gets harder and harder, it gets harder and harder to stand. His legs shake and feel numb. Random images roll through his mind: Wren, a Nav, food, Marilyn, but none of them clear. He's watching them through a tinted window, unable to reach for them. And that's it. Then it goes dark. He's a wooden plank falling to the ground.

The world fades away.

And his back hits the hard floor.

As it all fades away.

* * *

Marilyn's grip on the gun falters, then tightens til her forefinger is almost flexed on the trigger again. "Victor?" She tries calling out. But he lays shaking, trembling on the ground.

She aims her sight at Flannel, who brings himself slowly to his feet to find a barrel breathing into his face. He stands up, arms raised. "Put the gun down, girl." He makes a step toward her. She feels the gun tempting her to shoot. Taunting. And he takes another step.

"Stay." She snaps, like she's talking to a dog. Like a dog, he obeys.

How could he not?

"I don't know what got into him, it's got nothing to do with me, he's just my gardener." Flannel points to the upturned lifeless body of the gardener staring at the ceiling, arms strewn awkwardly across his chest. The syringe still gleaming beside him.

"You were going to shoot him." She says. And she tries to say Victor. "Why?"

Flannel sighs. "I can't say." And steps come from upstairs. Pacing. Crying. The ceiling creaks from the second floor.

"What is that?" She demands.

"What is what?"

"The needle. What is it?"

But he doesn't answer. He sighs.

Marilyn takes a few cautious steps toward it, the gardener's corpse, keeping the gun locked onto Flannel. She crouches slowly to get it, then walks over to Victor. She tries shaking him, never taking her eyes off the farmer.

"What happened to him?"

"I told you, it's got nothing to do with me!"

"Did this guy work for you?"

"Yes, I told you, he was our gardener, but—"

"Then it's got something to do with you! Get him some medicine!"

"I don't even know what it is he's got!"

He's not listening. Marilyn's hands are shaking. She's been around guns, but she's never had to fire one. She's never had to take aim at a living breathing person. And it's eating at her from the inside. It still doesn't feel real.

She looks back at Flannel and wonders, *What would Victor do?* And she thinks. And she knows. And she's afraid of it. Her teeth grit and it all comes flooding out, all at once, coursing through her body, into her fingers, and out the barrel of the gun.

The shotgun roars. Thin slivers of smoke puff from the barrel, and she can feel the heat of the bullet's aftermath as it flies into the wall. Flannel lets out a yell. He stands wide-eyed, fingers shaking. *Now he'll listen.*

Marilyn shoots him a steel-eyed glare. "Medicine. Now." It's almost a whisper. A powerful whisper.

Flannel shakes away the shock from almost having his head blown off. But not the fear. Marilyn knows he would not shake off the fear as long as she had this gun in her hands. He scrambles off into the kitchen. Marilyn follows him. He opens a cabinet full of pill-filled containers. The rattle of the medicine fills the cabinet as Flannel's shaky hands shove several bottles out of the way. He lines up smelling salts and different kinds of shock-inducing pills for heart failure.

The problem is, if Victor is alive, what to give him to keep him that way.

Then, Flannel looks over a medicine bottle. He reads the label and puts it back in the cabinet quickly.

"What was that?" Marilyn shakes the gun.

"Nothing."

A shameless lie.

"What was in that bottle?"

"Nothing."

Marilyn raises the shotgun again, making the man hesitate. His eyes are bloodshot, but what can a man do, for all the anger in the world, against a woman aiming a gun at his chest.

"They're for my wife. They make her walk again for a few hours. It brings back the functions or something."

She puts away the sting of sudden guilt she feels. "All the functions?"

"I don't know how it works."

Marilyn takes the bottle and hurries back to kneel over Victor. She takes one of the pills out. A tiny half-solid-black, half-semi-transparent-gray pill. She drags him to recline his back against the wall. He looks like he's asleep, but a breathless sleep. A dead sleep. And she realizes how calm he looks. How still. She pushes the thoughts away, suppressing whatever it is about that thought that makes her stomach churn.

She slips the pill into his mouth and prays that it works. His semi-deadness thankfully doesn't prevent the pill from going through. She waits.

"How long does it take for it to work?" She asks, looking at Victor's eyes.

She hears Flannel answer, "A few minutes." Silently.

Marilyn watches Victor's face anxiously, hoping for a sign of life. Hoping for him to open his eyes. She watches him.

But nothing happens. She can't hear breath anymore. She can't hear a heartbeat. To her surprise, her shoulders drop, and she finds herself breathless. She nestles her head on Victor's shoulder. "No." She whispers to no one in particular. "No." She rests on Victor's torn and smeared jacket.

And suddenly, she hears something. A thump. A beat. She curses herself for imagining things. But it happens again. Another beat. She looks up. She can see Victor's chest rising and falling. A spark of adrenaline fires through her veins.

"The smelling salts." She says to herself. And she fumbles through the medicines to find them. The little tube of smelling salts.

She places them under his nose. And she watches him.

And she forgets to watch Flannel.

He jumps in from behind and pulls at the shotgun with both hands, tearing Marilyn away from Victor.

She kicks at him, but he's quick to dodge. Flannel pushes and pulls at the gun, and he moves his hands toward Marilyn's. His nails dig into her fingers, and she wants to let go.

And she hears a click. The gun loses all the weight of struggle. Flannel lifts his hands, snarling.

Because there's a gun at his head.

"Get up."

Flannel stands up, leaving Marilyn on the floor.

And Victor stands beside him, not turning to look at Marilyn. But he says, "Marilyn, tie him up."

She gets up and looks for a rope.

Flannel sits down on the chair Victor pulls out for him. Crestfallen. Defeated.

* * *

Victor takes in a couple of breaths through his nose. For a moment after waking up, he had wondered where he was. How he got there. But now he remembers.

Everything hurts. It's like the adrenaline in him became

sharp and cuts through his body, singeing its way along the course of his veins.

It hurts to hold up the gun, but he has to. Before he loses ground again. He feels a numbness run down half of his body and a sting throughout the other side. And he takes a silent breath.

"Victor?" Marilyn is back with the rope. She's still confused, and he can't explain it any better than she can.

"Tie him up, please." He tells her.

"You're alive." She shows the slightest hints of a smile.

Victor doesn't smile back. He can't let the weakness show. A burst of pain like pins stabbing him runs through his limbs and back, but he grits his way through it.

"Tie him up, quick." He feels the gun weighing down on his arm.

Marilyn wraps the rope around the farmer. She makes a tight knot.

Flannel sits desperately.

Victor lets himself feel the pain, and he relaxes his arms, almost falling to the ground. Marilyn rushes to help him up.

"I changed my mind," he winces from the blood-rushing, "Just kill me now."

"You'll be fine," Flannel says, "That's just the meds taking effect."

Victor turns to see the gardener sprawled out on the floor, bugs starting to crowd around his chest. He sees Marilyn swallow, and he lifts the gun back toward Flannel. "You tried to kill me."

"I had nothing to do with it!"

"You're about one lie away from a bullet in your leg."

Flannel sneers, "I'm just trying to get you all out of my house.

Away from my family."

The gun pulses. And it hesitates. His finger moves away from the trigger.

"Your family. They're still upstairs?"

Marilyn shifts. She disappears into the kitchen. Victor hears footsteps upstairs.

Flannel nods.

"Call out to them. They're probably worried."

Flannel doesn't shift his eyes away from Victor. "Kids! Olive! Stay upstairs! Whatever you hear, don't come down!"

Marilyn comes back with a bottle of pills. "Take these. Painkillers." Her voice sounds distant. Like a ghost of a whisper. An echo of a thought.

She passes him two little pills, which he pops into his mouth without even waiting for a glass of water. He exhales the pain, feeling as it washes through him and out of him, almost taking his energy with it.

It's late, the sun is almost hiding behind the hills, buried by the shadow. If this planet has a moon, it should be peeking its pale head out about now. It's late. He doesn't know the time difference between this planet and Urbis, but anything might be too late, which means they have to leave, which means they have to move, which means a storm of pain even with the painkillers taking effect.

Victor braces himself and walks toward Flannel. But his foot kicks against something. And there's a rattle at his feet. The little clear tube rolls across the floor, and returns to him, still spinning, its yellowish liquid sloshing around in crests. Victor picks it up and raises it to the light. A beam of yellowish light falls to the floor. He takes the tube and raises it to Flannel's eye.

"Do you know what this is?"

"I've never seen it." There's no usual traces of a lie.

Victor slides it back into his pocket.

"I need to make a call." He says, "Do you have a phone?"

Flannel reluctantly nods toward a little room through a hall. Victor walks past the doors and into a small room with a phone hanging on the wall. He shuts himself in. The only light is from a lamp beside a small table. He sits down, feeling his pain creep back in.

The phone is an old version of the pay phone in Egeria. Victor clicks in the number. The room is stuffy, and clouds of dust breathe through the room, moving in waves, sticking to everything and anything. The line clicks.

"Royce residence."

"Hey, Mrs. Royce, is your husband there by any chance?"

"Who is this?" The voice on the other end sounds kind, gentle, but precise.

"It's Victor, I need to talk to your husband, please."

"Victor, is everything alright?"

"It's alright, Mrs. Royce, I just need to talk to your husband."

"Sure, I'll put him on."

A moment passes before the line clicks again, and an old, familiar voice, like the scratch of an old record in an antique store, comes through the receiver.

"Mr. Wolff?"

"Hans, I need your help, I'm flying in tonight, I need a ride."

"Of course, sir, but I'm afraid I will not be able to assist you as a driver tonight. I have a toothache, you see..."

Toothache...

Victor puts the phone down for a second, mutters to himself and waves off the dust building up on his forehead. The room feels suddenly that much more cramped.

"Does it hurt that much?"

"*It's more painful than you can imagine.*"

"The front teeth?"

"*Molars, sir. But I'm afraid I can't leave without them aching...*"

"Well," Victor exhales, scattering the dust particles in the yellowish light, "That's a shame."

"*Is something wrong, sir?*"

Victor can't help but wince. There's something about the old chauffeur's voice that fills him with nostalgia. "Too much to count, Hans. I'll tell you when I see you."

"*Good luck, sir.*"

Victor thanks Hans. And the room empties silently. There's no hum at the end of the record. Just a quiet, dust-ridden room.

He walks back through the corridor.

And Flannel blocks his way back to the living room, pointing a dusty old revolver at his head. "I can't let you leave until you tell me what's going on."

Victor doesn't feel fear at the old revolver. Because he's pointing his own gun back at the giant barring the hall.

"You first." He feels his old voice come back, the rust washed off by the prospect of semi-death. He looks at the toy of a gun.

"All I know is a guy comes to threaten my family, says if I see a young boy about nineteen years old, I'm to step out of the way, let him into my house, and leave the rest up to the gardener." Flannel says, clicking the hammer back.

"But you got a shootout instead."

"I told you, I'm just trying to keep my family safe. Who are you?"

"Try this on for size, Flannel. I'm a very important person with very important friends, and very important ex-friends.

These ex-friends own everything except for the few things they don't. Now, some of the few things they don't own are me and Marilyn. And some of the many things they do own are you, your family, and your farm, so if there's anyone you shouldn't be pointing that gun at, it's me."

"I want you out of my house."

"Where's Marilyn?"

"Upstairs."

"We're not bad people."

"There's a body in my living room. Good people don't leave bodies behind with bullets in their chests."

Victor feels the weight of the words pressing against him, crushing him if he falters for a moment. And he feels the truth in them. But it's not like he had a choice, if he didn't pull that trigger, he would've died. It was him or the gardener. So he answers, "We're not as bad as them."

"Who are you?" The boiler of Flannel' voice groans again.

Victor smiles. "I'm Victor Wolff."

There's a silence. A choking silence. And he knows what comes next.

Flannel's eyes don't shift away, but the revolver lowers to his side. "Are you gonna kill him?"

"I don't want to."

"Are you gonna *stop* him?" Flannel clarifies, annoyed.

Victor's eyes narrow. As much as he wants to answer, the words get caught in his throat for a split second. The question makes his stomach tighten and the gears start turning in his head. But there's no time for gear-turning. And he sees only one way to answer the question. And he thinks: *Never let them see your fear.* Victor smirks slightly. "Count on it."

Flannel turns his eyes to the floor and nods. "I want my

family safe."

"I'll do you one better: how about your family free?"

"What do you need?"

"We need a ride. And lunch."

Flannel nods.

"Thanks, pal."

Flannel scoffs.

The day is wearing thin. The sun is digging its way into the ground. The dusk hits the little farm like a streak of paint, bathing it in humid heat and orange brushstrokes, and sending burps of steam evaporating in the air. A fog with drops drizzling like stars unfurling onto the ground.

Victor limps over to Marilyn, who's looking out the window at nature's cry for attention.

As soon as Victor takes a first step into the room, she turns around, cautious hope in her eyes.

"How are they?" He asks.

"They were scared. But they're alright. I'm sorry."

Victor nods.

And she asks, "Do we have a ride?"

"We have a ride."

"Do we have a plan?"

His lips curve into a smile. It's as if no one knows him. Everyone always asks the same question. Everyone always gets the same answer. "We have a plan."

14

The medicines rattle as she throws them into the pack. She packs the bag with essentials. Medicines. Food. But no gun. The gun is on the table behind her. She can't bear to look at it. Can't bear to hold it. But Victor insists.

She zips the bag and looks back, taking in the space. She was given a room to get ready in, alone, far from the noise. The farm is quiet, so quiet she can hear her own breathing. The voice of the evening comes and goes in whispers. Breeze. Hush. Howl. Hush.

And it scares her.

She's never known this kind of quiet. Her childhood lullabies were the sounds of sirens and the yelling of the cars on the street. She remembers the distinct tone car horns have in the night. Tired, long screams. Angry screams. But now she can hear her own breathing.

And it scares her.

* * *

Victor walks into her room, he watches her listening to the night. And he wonders, *what does she hear?*

Because all he hears is the voice of a species of wolf or coyote at its night hunt. He imagines it creeping up to house.

But she seems to hear something different. And she doesn't notice him sit beside her.

"Are you okay?"

She shakes her head and looks down at her feet. Her fists are clenched. Victor tries to read her expression, but it's something he doesn't quite recognize.

"We're gonna be okay. We're gonna see the end of this." He says. And he worries it might not be the right thing to say.

"But through whose eyes?" She asks.

"What do you mean?"

"I fired the gun, Victor. I killed him back there."

He understands. But he doesn't feel. He hates the emptiness that grows in him like a bubble of nothingness expanding in his core.

And she goes on.

"Who are we gonna be when this is all over?"

He doesn't answer. He doesn't know how.

"What if we're just like him?"

He wants her to stop. Stop.

"What if this is how he started? One life. Then two. Then more."

Stop.

"We can't become him, Victor. We have to stop."

Stop.

"*You* have to stop."

Please, stop.

"We can't win like this... Not like this."

He gets up and walks away, leaving her alone in her silence. With the wolves. Looking for their prey.

And he leaves. He barges out the door and sits on the steps.

And he shakes. His hands shiver as a deep cold spreads through him, freezing his blood. He feels a pull, gripping at his lungs, squeezing the breath out of him, suffocating. Suffocating. And the gun weighing heavier and heavier in his pocket. Clicking in his mind. Firing. Firing. Round after round. And he can't get it out of his head. The sound. The bullet. The smoke. And the body in the living room. Dead.

He can't take it.

He wants it to stop.

Stop.

Stop.

But it thrums repetitively. And a ringing in his ears. And a ringing in the house. And a click.

"You have to stop."

And she's looking at him. He feels the tube of yellowish liquid in his pocket. And he says, "We have to go." But he leaves the tube on the windowsill.

Flannel walks out of the house first. Victor follows beside Marilyn. Every step kicks up the moisture on the grass. Victor feels the drizzle building up droplets in his hair. He runs a hand through it to shake off the water.

They follow Flannel into a garage with a rusted blue pickup truck with mud on the wheels parked at a crooked angle.

Victor stares at Flannel's back. Without turning, Flannel asks, "How old are you two?"

Wolff tries looking at the man's expression through the mirror of the truck, but it's too far away.

"Why do—"

"Nineteen." Marilyn answers before he can lie.

Victor shoots her a glare, but regrets it immediately. She

outglares him.

"You're just kids?" Flannel poses it as a question but it comes out as more of a statement, like he's telling them rather than asking. Victor feels the bitterness of it, but he hides it. He always hides it. People are more willing to cooperate with a smile than a frown. Let *them* get angry. A furious mind destroys itself. It will starve if you don't feed it. *Don't feed it,* Victor reminds himself. And he hears the echo of Wren's voice in his head. He hates it.

Victor opens the door for Marilyn as Flannel gets into the car, then he goes around the back. The trunk of the pickup is covered by a tarp, but it lays loosely over the items beneath it. One of them is in the shape of a shotgun.

How many guns does this guy own?

Victor takes a look around and reaches his hand into the tarp, fingering around for the gun. He ducks behind the trunk, opens the cartridge and pulls the bullets out. If it comes to it, he doesn't know that he can go up against a shotgun again.

"Let's go!"

Victor almost jumps. He slides the bullets into his pocket and puts the shotgun back in the trunk. Wolff falls back into his walk around the trunk and jumps in the passenger seat.

"What took you so long?"

Victor smiles at the suspicion in Flannel's eyes. "Just a kid doing kid stuff." He catches Marilyn looking back and forth from him to Flannel. Apparently, Flannel notices too.

"Alright," He clicks his tongue, "Astroport, then."

The truck's engine starts, the air condition pants out like it's been holding in a breath for too long, and the wheels start turning, and the windows roll up, and a cloud of dust blows up around them as the pickup kicks away from the house, which gets smaller and smaller by the minute. And a woman and her kids looking out the window.

The open road is boring to look at. Grass here. More grass over there. What's that over there? It's grass. Plus the odd bald patch or a tree. The truck is cooler now that it's picking up speed. About sixty miles per hour. It's still not very fast, but apparently Flannel is really pushing the gas. And all that pushing finally leads to a puff of the motor. And a brake. And a rattle inside the car which sends all their heads flying forward. The truck strains forward making a dying effort to start again. Then it dies.

Victor checks his watch and groans. This had to happen. Now.

"Gas is out." Flannel is so kind to point out, since Victor had apparently not seemed to notice the car isn't moving anymore.

"You don't say..."

"Is there a gas station nearby?" Marilyn sighs, kind as ever.

Flannel clicks open his door. "Yeah, we're gonna have to push, though."

"You don't say..." Victor swings open the door and walks to the back, where Flannel is already getting ready to push.

And he pulls the shotgun out of the trunk.

"What's that for?" Marilyn asks.

Flannel slings the gun around his back with a makeshift rope strap. His ears prick up and he takes a slow look around. And he whispers, "Just in case..."

And Victor feels the bullets in his pocket.

"On the count of three we push." Flannel says. He points at Marilyn and says, "You're going to have to steer."

He counts. One. And the full force of the wind blows back on them. Two. And the grass whips on the sides. Three. And they push. The truck lurches forward, and pretty soon it's moving slowly down the road.

They haven't even pushed half a mile when they came to a gas station. A rusty old building made from cheap metal and two little pumps. A black van is already driving into one of them. Victor and Flannel push the car onto the station beside the other pump.

"I got it from here." Flannel says. Victor doesn't want to let him out of his sight, but his legs are killing him. The sweat is beading up on his forehead and dripping down his neck. He drags himself back into the already-humid car, watches Flannel carry the pump to the truck. Everything about this man says he can't be trusted. That he'll do anything in his power to make sure Victor never comes near his planet again. He doesn't act on it, but he will. He will.

"You think we can trust him?" Marilyn's voice makes a rift through the silence from the back seat.

"I don't think we can trust anyone."

"I don't think we have a choice."

"That's why I take precautions."

"What precautions?" She asks gravely.

"Don't worry about it."

And the bullets remind him of his own gun. He takes his handgun out and reloads it with some of the rounds in his pack. And the mirror is nothing but sky when he raises his head again.

"Victor, where is he?"

Flannel is gone. Victor peers into the rearview mirror, and there he is, walking around with the shotgun in his hands.

I knew it. Victor cocks his gun and keeps it close to his body, waiting. Waiting. But Flannel never comes back. Instead, he goes the other way. "Where's he going?"

And a man in a track suit gets out of the passenger seat of the black van, the shadow of a driver disappearing as he shuts the door behind him.

Flannel faces Track Suit, with the shotgun strapped around his shoulder. They're talking, but Victor can't make out the words. Track Suit's eyes look beady behind his thin rimmed glasses. And everything about him screams Urbis. And everything about him screams goon. Wren's goon. Goons. Another one comes out of the back seat, a pistol outlined in his pocket, where his hand is, and he looks over to the truck.

Victor ducks out of sight, hearing the scrape of the back seat and Marilyn doing the same. Footsteps crackle on the rocky asphalt, getting louder with every crunch. Closer. Wolff puts his gun between his knees, aims at the door. But the man's face appears at the window, and the face of a gun stares him down, aimed between his eyes. Surprise is written all over the goon's eyes.

That's when Victor kicks the door open, smacking the window into the man's face. Wolff leaps to his feet, his pistol aimed at the man's head, but he's already unconscious. He shifts his aim to Track Suit. Behind him, the van is backing out of the gas station.

And the same look of surprise marks Track Suit's face when he sees Victor. "Aren't you supposed to be dead?" And he glares at Flannel.

And Flannel still has his shotgun primed.

"I guess I didn't get the memo." Victor's grip tightens around the pistol. And he sees Flannel ready to shoot nothing but air.

"We can fix that." Track Suit fires his gun.

Victor ducks just in time to feel the bullet fly past his right ear and strike whatever is behind him. A shrill hiss fills the air. Wolff checks himself for blood and sees Track Suit raising his pistol to shoot again. And there's a boom that breaks the atmosphere. And Victor barrels at him, knocking Track Suit onto the pavement.

The gun flies out of Track Suit's hand. Wolff jumps into a run and kicks it away. And he takes aim. And he sees Marilyn looking at him. He sees the fear. And he walks back, picks up the gun.

But Flannel is lying on the ground behind him, his shotgun gone. And Track Suit is already standing over him, shotgun ready to shoot.

He sees Flannel's face, eyebrows turned up in an expression that can only mean one thing.

A hiss and a strong smell of gasoline.

And it can only mean "RUN."

Track Suit catches the glance and turns his gun to Flannel, threatening to shoot, but Flannel's mouth is already bleeding, and his chest has a bullet buried too deep for him to stand, and he has a revolver hidden in his red flannel plaid shirt, the silver gleams in his hand. He pulls back the hammer.

Victor sees the gun and runs toward the truck, leaving Flannel behind because he knows there's no way he can carry him, leaving Track Suit behind. Leaving dust trailing behind. And gripping the steering wheel. He stomps on the accelerator and the truck pushes off backwards, falling back onto the road.

"What's happening!" Marilyn is hanging on to the front seat, trying to click the seat belt into place.

"Wren."

"Why?"

"To make sure the job was finished."

After a fraction of a second she connects the dots. "The gardener."

"The dead gardener. He probably called them, took precautions."

"Where are we going now?"

And she keeps asking questions, but there's something gnawing at him from the inside and he hates the way it's blurring his thoughts. But he answers, "Same place that guy's going. Astroport." He points to the black van in the distance.

"What about Mark?"

"Who?" He connects the dots and brakes. Flannel is standing up against a trigger-happy goon in a track suit whose gun is just aching to shoot something. But it wouldn't shoot. And at least Victor gave him that.

They get out of the car and hear the gunfire. And they see Track Suit fumbling and then falling back. And it's all gone in a flash of smoke and fire. A blast in the sky sucks up all the air. All the sound. The sky blackens with ash. A high pitched shriek and a roar of flame.

And Marilyn is crying as fire rises up like a dragon to consume what remains of the gas station. What remains of Track Suit. And What remains of Flannel. Mark. And there's nothing to be done.

"We can't go back." Victor tells her. But he feels the weight of his guilt. And he locks it away. Because the guilt is a fear.

I couldn't have carried him. And he had a bullet in his chest.

"I'm sorry, we can't go back for him, I'm sorry." And he is. But his stomach tightens anyway, and a gulp runs down his throat, filling him with the taste of smoke and the smell of gas is rancid in the air. "I'm sorry."

We can't go back.

Those words echo in the silence that follows the explosion. The ringing in his ears. The silence that holds him by the throat.

And it holds them when they get back into the truck.

And it holds them when they drive away, the flame tracing a line into the sky behind them.

And it holds them when he looks at Marilyn.

Because the weight of the guilt is getting heavier. And she doesn't know it.

Because the weight is getting heavier, just like the weight of the bullets in his pocket.

The bullets that belong to the shotgun that belongs to the man who just saved their lives.

But the silence vanishes when they cross the bridge into the parking garage of the Astroport. People rush into the Astroport, rush through security, rush out of security.

Victor parks far away enough from the building that no wandering Astroport security guard might be tempted to check the truck and report it stolen.

"We can't get through security with a bunch of guns." Marilyn says.

Victor takes the shotgun bullets out of his pocket and hides them in the glove compartment. And he empties his gun, too.

"How do you think I've gotten this far? This is Wren's gun, which means I have a permit for it, which means as long as it's empty, I'm cleared."

"You think we'll make it before Wren finds out we're still alive?" She's tying her hair up with a rubber band she found somewhere on the ground.

"I hope so, but I don't want to find out the hard way. You think that's sanitary?"

"What?"

"I said, do you think that's sanitary?"

"The band?"

"Yeah, the floor band."

"I think sanitary is the least of our problems."

"I don't think getting sick on this trip is worth the risk."

"I've lived through worse." Marilyn takes her pack and shuts the door.

Victor just turns back to the building, clearing his throat.

"Um, we should get going." *Um?* The word, if it can even be considered a word, feels like foreign medicine in his mouth. He curses himself for letting *um* get away from him.

And he carries *um* through the revolving doors, looking around for the driver of the black van. Victor hadn't gotten a good look at him, but Wren's goons tend to stick out. And there he is, like a sore thumb walking through security in a black pinstripe suit over a black turtleneck, a black suitcase in his hand and an expensive looking black matte watch around his wrist. He's looking around warily.

"There he is." Marilyn whispers. Victor nods back.

They cross security behind him, keeping him always in their sights. After crossing, the man waits at the terminal. Victor hides behind a newspaper. The terminal is laid out in a way that the waiting seats are lined up on one side of the walkway and the shops on the other side, lined up all the way to the doors leading to the narrow strips of AstroNav loading docks.

"We can't let him get away." Victor whispers through the aisle of Sawmill keychains.

"We can't just knock him out here." Marilyn whispers back, only here eyes are visible through the slot between the shelves.

"If he gets to Wren, none of this works. He can't know I'm

alive or he'll be on his guard."

"So we have to knock him out here."

"Not here."

"What?"

"I have an idea."

"Oh. Should I be worried?"

"Just keep your eye on him. Don't move." Victor walks out of the aisle, keeping check of the man from behind the cap he bought at the gift shop, a big red "Vacation in Sawmill!"

The flight attendants are sitting around the terminal, waiting for the Navs to start boarding. Waiting for the pilot, looking at their watches. Waiting for someone to ask a question.

"Excuse me."

The redhead flight attendant looks up with a bored stare.

"I need your help with something."

"Yes, sir? What can I help you with?" She recites with the fakest smile Victor's ever seen.

"What's your name?"

"Georgia."

"What a coincidence, I'm George Hill." He pulls out a few bills from his wallet, and then her smile is real, "Listen, Georgia, you have two doors..."

The doors of the elevator open. Victor looks around but can't catch a glimpse of the goon. And the crowd starts moving in a straight line. Victor keeps his head down, looking at the ground, acting like he's just watching his step. He bumps shoulders, making the passengers turn to look at him, but none of them look familiar.

Marilyn walks the same way, right in front of him. They take their seats at the end of the row in the coach section of the

Nav. And the Nav takes off, impatiently as always. The rings begin to spin out the window, and the AstroNav rises above the clouds, and the sky becomes pitch black, sprinkled by tiny gleams across its vast expanse—a sea of stars.

Marilyn shifts in her seat, her blue eyes still have a distant look to them, "What exactly did you do?"

"I told you."

"Got the flight attendant to smile isn't an answer."

"Calm down, it'll work."

And Georgia walks up after a few minutes. "It's all set, Mr. Hill."

"Great," Victor says, standing up.

She hesitates, "What exactly are you going to do?"

Victor cracks a smirk, "And here I thought we trusted each other."

Marilyn scoffs, but the flight attendant just shrugs and nods. She leads them to a little cabin, with a closet and a curtain over the window.

"Here you are."

"Perfect. Thank you, Georgia."

"Mhm." She walks out of the room. He can almost see her counting the money in her head.

"What now?" Marilyn asks as soon as the door clicks shut.

"Now, our friend Georgia is gonna tell Mr. Driver, that Mr. Wren has paid for his cabin in first class."

"What do *we* do?"

"For now, hide." Victor disappears into the shadows of the curtain. The little room comes with a bed and a dimmed light, darker than most Nav cabin lights, which the man is sure to notice, but by then it would be too late.

And the darkness is only interrupted by a crack in the closet door.

The cabin door clicks. It slides open, letting in a beam of light. Then it slides shut again. The man had managed to smuggle a gun through security, most likely with the same kind of Wren permit. And he's fingering the gun. He sticks his hand in his other pocket and lifts a silencer to his eyes. He examines it carefully, like a science, and screws it onto the front of his pistol. Victor primes his movements, plans them out carefully. He can feel his heart pulsing, mixing in with the quiet footsteps in the room. He watches, ready to attack, claws drawn, blood pumping, pulse quickening, but eyes focused and keen, not letting one movement escape him.

And the moment comes.

The sound comes from the closet, the man turns to look, and Victor pounces.

His fist flies into the man's cheek, hitting bone and muscle. Wolff gets his balance back while the man stumbles. He throws all his weight onto the driver, and Marilyn jumps out of the closet, holding the man back. She moves her fingers to the back of the goon's neck and presses down. The man struggles against Victor's weight, but his strength drains out of him, and he falls unconscious. His legs give out and Victor lowers him to the ground.

He takes a handkerchief from the man's pocket and grabs the gun.

And Marilyn pulls him back, "You can't kill him."

Victor hesitates. He wasn't going to. He wasn't. He nods.

But doesn't answer. He pulls out some zip ties and wraps them around the man's hands and feet, carefully avoiding the matte watch.

"Georgia will make sure he catches the next flight all the

way to Egeria. He'll be arrested there for smuggling weapons. Hopefully, the Emperor will take it as a peace offering. Or a warning. I don't care."

"How'd you know he had a gun?"

"*I* always did." He lays down on the bed, feeling Marilyn still staring at him. And he feels the guilt eating him up. And he hides it. He always hides it. And he feels the weight of his gun. *I always do.*

* * *

He seems so calm. He just tied someone up in a closet, and he seems so calm.

Marilyn's legs give out, and she sits down on the bed. She stares at her feet, not looking, just thinking. Thinking of the fire. The smoke. And the children waiting for their father to come home.

But Victor seems calm. Careless.

And she says it to him again, "You can't be like him."

Victor's eyes open. "I told you. I'm not like him."

"Victor, I shot him. I shot the gardener, and it's been destroying me, but you've done so much more, and you're sleeping."

And he sits up, "I'm doing what I have to do to keep us alive."

He says it calmly. So calmly it scares her.

"When I fired that gun, I felt it carry me. Like it wasn't me shooting, but it was. And I don't know if you forget that or if you just don't care, but it's *you* who's shooting. Not the gun."

"What do you want me to do?"

"I want you to stop. If we make it to the end of this, we can't be monsters like him."

He sits watching her. Observing. And he answers. "I'm not the same kind of monster."

And she sees the crack in the facade. For a split second, he lets her see through the mask.

And it scares her.

"I'm not him," He says, "I promise."

And he smiles at her. But she can't tell if it's him or the mask.

15

He hears the sound of pacing. Footsteps moving around the room.

He hears his voice. Wren's voice.

And he says, "Never let them see your fear, kid."

He's pacing, wondering, thinking. "Where'd you go, Victor?"

"Who killed you, Victor?"

Footsteps.

"Was it the pit or the venom?"

Victor tries to shake himself awake. Because he knows it's a dream. It can't be real. But he's in the room. He's in the room with Adolf Wren.

"Was it the venom or the farmer you let die. The farmer you killed."

And he thinks of Flannel. Mark. And how he died. *I couldn't have carried him.*

But he can't say that out loud.

"Was it the farmer or the fear?"

And he can't take it and he shuts his eyes. And he opens them.

And he's not there anymore. But he hears pacing.

Marilyn is walking back and forth. She's staring at the closet.

He sits up. "Do you wanna go back?"

She spins around startled. Still recovering, she asks, "What?"

"Back to our seats."

"Oh, yeah."

Victor nods and follows her back to their seats. They leave the unconscious body in the closet behind them, letting all the light leave the room with them.

"I'll be right back." He says to Marilyn.

And he leaves her in the seat. He doesn't know if she heard him. And he thinks grimly:

Was it the pit that killed her or the gun? Or the fear?

But he walks. All the way to the front of the Nav, behind the curtain, watching people watch him.

He puts the handkerchief on the table. Georgia stares at it from behind fear-glazed eyes.

"Look, you'll be fine, just don't open it, don't touch it without the handkerchief."

But she's not listening. She's frozen.

He sighs. There's nothing left to do but hope. "Just don't let him out before Egeria. And don't tell anyone. Please. Don't let them see your fear."

Nothing.

He smiles. "It's alright. I'll handle it." And he leaves the handkerchief along with a few bills and a packet of pretzels.

He walks back through the diminished curiosity of the passengers and sits down at his seat. Marilyn avoids his gaze. And *um* keeps coming to mind. And he curses himself for *um*.

After the longest flight of his life, the Nav finally hovers over the Astroport of Urbis, landing on the planet. Wren's planet. *My planet.* But it feels different.

He doesn't quite remember leaving. He feels like he's been here the whole time. But he hasn't. And here the night is young. Still, he smiles because it's home.

They walk through the doors of the Astroport, stepping onto the sidewalk.

Marilyn wipes away the last traces of a sandwich Victor had bought at a bagel place at the Astroport. Victor had one too, but his wasn't even half-finished. Somehow, he doesn't feel so hungry anymore. The bagel was more of an early victory gift to himself. It reminds him of a bagel place off the corner of Wren's citadel, an old farmer-turned-city-woman with a thick accent. The bagels from there are better. And the lady is also a good informant for Wren, so it's no surprise that she has the least artificial produce. And it's no surprise that she's only one of the many informants Wren has around the planet.

"Victor," Marilyn is look at him, a fresh hint of something in her eyes, "You haven't told me the plan. Or if it'll work."

"Do you trust me?"

She turns away from him, chucking the newspaper-design wrapping paper of the bagel into a trash can. Looking toward the street she mutters, and he can feel the hesitation in her voice. "Yes."

"Good," He says, taking a bite out of the bagel.

The bright lights hide the night. The few stars you can see are constellations, the names of which Victor can never remember. "How do people name those things?"

"What things?" Marilyn is looking at the lights, not the stars.

"The constellations, that one doesn't look like anything to me."

"That one's Tyche," She says, a smile brightening her eyes.

"It's named after the goddess of luck."

"Huh," Victor realizes he's never heard that one before.

Wren wasn't so sentimental as to look up at the stars. And

at school, his professors had never taught him much about the sky. "You know, my teachers used to tell me not to focus too much on the sky. And Wren used to say, 'We have enough problems on the ground, without looking up at the sky.'"

"Isn't looking at the sky what got us here?"

He can't help turning to look at her. She's looking up at the sky with true wonder in her eyes. He turns back to the stars, cursing himself for *um*, but he can't focus on Tyche anymore.

"We should go before someone sees us."

The slightest and briefest hint of disappointment flutters across Marilyn's face, but she looks around at the people flowing out of the Astroport, "Yeah, we should go."

A taxi finally comes to a stop, coming to rest right in front of them. But the windows are tinted, and he can't see the driver through the glass.

He waves the cab along. He can't risk taking a taxi. Just like he can't risk buying a decent bagel.

Victor leads Marilyn across the parking lot.

"You think Wren's men will be looking out for us?" Marilyn asks.

"His spy didn't get back to him, but I don't think he'll let that ruffle his feathers. It's The Source I'm worried about."

"She's after Wren, not us."

"That's not the way she sees it. If she can get us out of the way, she will."

He takes a turn at the first alley. Walking in the open would be too risky in their shape. Their clothes are grimy, Victor's suit is torn at the shoulder and he'd ditched his tie somewhere along the way, even though he can't remember taking it off. Marilyn looks a bit better, but her hair is messy, her light makeup smeared, and her clothes altogether wrinkled and stained by all kinds of stuff. Not to mention the lingering smell of smoke and gasoline.

The back way is impossible to get through quickly. There are too many pipes, brick walls, rats, and something that smells worse than they do.

Marilyn pulls away from Victor and steps out of the alley. Victor rushes out after her. The sidewalk is saturated with walking zombies, noses stuck in their own business. He sees Marilyn already taking her chances and mixing in with the people, looking back to make sure Victor's following.

He takes a sigh, she looks pretty much like a goldfish swimming in a school of sardines. Hopefully their noses are stuck in their business enough to not be able to smell either of them. He merges in with the sardines. Going in separately is probably safer, not much of a chance both of them would be caught. But then, what would he do if they caught her?

The man on his side bumps into him and looks up to excuse himself, but grimaces mid-apology, scrunching up his nose. "What happened to you?" He asks, unconsciously wiping his velvet shoulder with his hand as if some of the stink would get stained on it.

"A pit, a needle, a gas station, and a goddess of luck named Tice."

"Huh?"

Victor pushes through the crowd, feeling the man's eyes still glued on him. Finally, he catches up to Marilyn. "This is our turn."

"Right."

"We'll be out in the open." They stop at the corner, the light shining red for pedestrians.

The school of sardines stops simultaneously, synchronized as if they all functioned at the beat of the city, as black and white as the crosswalk.

"If one of Wren's informants sees us, that's the end of the line."

"How do we know if they're informants?"

"We don't. That's the point. Try not to let anyone see you."

The sign blinks a couple of times and turns white, a stick figure walking across it. Then an orange hand appears, counting down the time to walk and waving them on. A kid pulls at her mother's hand, "Mommy, we're gonna get run over, come on, we have ten seconds."

And they start walking. Victor feels the shadow of a thousand eyes on him, following his footsteps. He feels it stronger every time he turns his head, making sure they're not being tailed.

The orange hand stops waving. And the zero disappears leaving a red hand in its place.

And the world burns with the light of headlights. Victor jumps to push Marilyn out of the way. She yells and pushes out her hands. A screeching skid of tires drags toward her. The shining short hood of a blue minivan freezes inches from her outstretched hands. And Victor tumbles onto the corner of the sidewalk, holding her down. Onlooking sardines stop their mindless swimming to stare at the two grimy goldfish lying on the ground at the edge of the sidewalk.

A woman steps out of the minivan, tall and impossibly thin, she reaches out to help them, but freezes and tilts her head. She gasps, takes off back into her car. And the blue minivan drives out of sight.

Victor lets out a long breath, helping Marilyn up. He sees the people, staring confused at them, outraged at the distraction from their self-absorbed lives.

"They know we're here." Marilyn says it absently, eyes still frozen.

Her hands are shaking. He can see the worry radiating through her as the thought comes out. Victor pulls her onto the stairs of a library and sits her down on the steps, crouching beside her.

"Listen," But she doesn't look up, "Hey, listen, we're fine. You're fine. There's nothing they can do to us that we can't get out of, alright?"

She looks into his eyes. His voice falters, but he recovers for her sake.

"We'll be fine, let's just get to where we're going, and everything will be alright." He lifts Marilyn to her feet. And he wonders.

Who killed you, the venom or the fear?

"We're almost there."

They turn a corner up ahead and climb up a humble red-brick building surrounded by pink flowers planted behind a fence of closed up bushes. Victor clicks a button beside the glass door. A shrill buzz rings from a speaker on it, and voice promptly asks, "Who is it?"

"It's me..."

"Of course, sir..." The buzz stops abruptly and then sounds again, louder. The door clicks and a shower of yellow light comes raining down on them. The warmth of the building washes over them and fills their lungs when they open the door.

They climb the stairs to the top floor, and stand on a doormat, wiping their shoes as if it would help. And the door opens. And a toad-faced man in a gray sweater and a white shirt smiles at them from behind a white mustache and steps aside to let them in.

"Make yourself at home, I'll make tea."

"You don't have to." Marilyn says kindly.

"Please, Miss Finch, I insist." And a sincerity radiates off of him that makes her nod.

"You know each other?" Victor asks, gazing from one to the other.

Marilyn answers, "Everyone knows Hans."

Victor watches the old driver disappear into the kitchen. He's known Hans since he started working for Wren, almost two years ago. They had struck up a conversation about the city and Hans's home planet. Victor remembers it fondly. Like it was yesterday.

He never imagined Hans at home, he always seemed more of a life-on-the-road type of guy. But the apartment is not lavish or lavishly decorated. Victor supposes people become less materialistic as they get older, finding the true meaning of riches or something. Then again, some people lose sight of it all when it comes to money. For some reason, he feels he wouldn't get it.

Hans invites them to sit on a plaid-cushioned sofa. The room is quiet. There's sirens outside like there always is, people crowding around some accident, wishing for something, anything, to break them out of their boring routine. But inside Hans's apartment is like a different world, sealed off from the noise. It feels like a home.

They listen to the clattering of the kitchen. "Tea will be ready in a few minutes," Hans says, coming back to sit.

Victor's expression changes as he notes Hans's arched white

eyebrows. "I don't like the taste of tea. Must be kind of hard on that toothache of yours."

"Yes, it can be quite bitter."

"Is it strong?"

Marilyn looks back and forth from one to the other with an arched eyebrow of her own.

"Very, I'm afraid. Can you smell it yet?"

"In the teapot?"

The boiling water begins to whistle, sending a shiver up Victor's spine.

Hans comes back with cups and pours out the stream of steaming water into Marilyn's cup, and then Victor's. He puts out a trickle, then a longer stream, and another, wait, short, long, stop, dash, and so on until the cup is almost overflowing with tea. Victor watches the charade intently, but Hans is talking to Marilyn about the weather, the movies, and other trivialities with a careless air.

Marilyn had started out trying to ask Victor what he was talking about, but, before long, she gets the idea, and answers with, "It's a bit cold for my taste."

Victor decodes the message in his head.

Watching. Everywhere.

"Thank you, Hans." Marilyn says.

The toad-faced chauffeur nods smilingly, then turns back to Victor.

"Is it Earl Gray?" Wolff tries to hide the fear in his voice. Not even letting Hans hear it. But there's eyes everywhere, waiting.

"No, sir, I don't know what it is."

Victor sits back, letting himself breathe, and he takes a sip of the tea. "You were right, it's bitter. Not as bitter as it could be though."

"My wife bought it."

"How is Mrs. Hans? She still own that tailoring shop over on 6th?"

"She does, sir. She's there now... Hiding"

"What do you say we pay her a visit? I've been meaning to get a new suit. I don't think I'll be taking the tea though."

"Tea," Hans smiles, "Is a very hard thing to dispose of, unfortunately."

Marilyn clicks her tongue. She's putting together the pieces, Victor can tell.

Hans had already put on a wool coat and his chauffeur cap. He leads Victor and Marilyn out of the building through a back way to the apartment garages. The garage has a strong scent of smoke and cigarettes, and ashes are sprinkled here and there in places that look like ash trays, but aren't. A man sits smoking in his black car, looking in the rearview mirror. Victor catches a quick frown pass through his face. He takes note of the license plate.

The limo shines its lights, clicking the doors unlocked. Victor crouches in after Marilyn. The darkness of the limo folds over him, and the silence scares him. Because he feels the man in the black car watching him.

"Are they in there?" He's thinking of coded ways to say it, but the man is watching and there's no time.

"No, sir, I told them I had other clients who would not enjoy having their words recorded."

"You're the best Hans." And he means it. Hans may be getting old, but he's still more than just a chauffeur. His eyes are still keen and he's quick as a whip, and Victor wouldn't trade him for any younger driver if they paid him to do it. Only if Hans asked for retirement would he ever let the chauffeur go.

But that hadn't happened yet, if it ever would.

"Sir," Hans starts the car and eases it out of the garage. There's a chill from the air conditioning that gives the night an eerie feel, and the car rumbles down the street, and he goes on to say, "Some people arrived at my home not two days ago and placed cameras, thinking I hadn't noticed. They did not tell me whose they were." He waits a bit, "Sir, I have been told Mr. Wren wishes you dead."

"Lots of people wish me dead."

"Do these people wish you dead, sir?"

"I'd say they're not thrilled to see me alive."

"They're called The Source." Hans's eyes turn to Marilyn in the rearview as she goes on, "They wanted us to help them kill Wren."

"But now they know you're alive, ma'am."

"They probably already knew that." Victor answers.

"They almost ran me over on the way here."

"Doesn't matter, they're just an obstacle. Wren is who we're after."

"Pardon, sir?"

"You know the deal about Mrs. Crow a couple years back?"

Hans looks directly at Victor, which makes him shrink.

"No one could miss it, sir, and I'm sorry for your loss, Miss Finch." Marilyn bows her head, as if in respect of the memory of her mother.

"We're looking for the document she found. We don't know what it is, but it has something to do with the Newton Project."

"How are you going to retrieve it?"

"I have a plan, but I'm gonna need your help."

The limo stops at a red light, and they can see Wren's citadel in the distance, and they can see a parade of people walking past it, and a small parade of people walks in.

"What's going on?" Victor watches them in their lavish clothes, designer dresses with lace collars and all the gold money can buy and they're all walking to Wren's tower.

"I'm not sure, sir." Hans says, turning away.

And a man walks beside the car, and Victor knows who it is. And it means he knows who everyone else is too. And it means his plan won't work, because Wren won't be alone.

"This isn't gonna work. We need to go." He says, and he calculates.

Marilyn leans over to look, "What's not gonna work?"

Victor hides behind his hands. "He's not alone."

And he opens the door and steps out. Because it's not just him anymore. And it's not just Marilyn anymore. And it's not just the file anymore.

"Victor, what's going on?"

And he sees the car behind them, and he checks the plates. He gets back in the car.

"We're being tailed."

"That's not the same license plate from the garage." Marilyn says. And *um* whispers back, but he doesn't have time to curse himself for it.

"I know, it's just a feeling."

"What do you need, sir?" Hans takes a wrong turn, trying to speed up and lose the car.

"We need to get to Mrs. Hans, I might need that suit now."

"Sir?"

"Victor, what's wrong?"

And the voices are stacking up with the sirens, and the car horns, and the crowds, and the music, and the air.

Because it's not just them anymore.

"He's going to kill them all."

16

The limousine rumbles through the street, harsh streetlight gleaming off its shiny black reflection, like a mirror thinly painted over with ink. Dark, dark ink. And it spins and paints a distorted picture of moonlight and street signs.

And the reflection of a black car following them. Ink within ink. And it mirrors their movements.

Victor's stomach clenches with a sudden nausea from watching the world spin like a record around him. And the distance between the two cars shrinks.

Marilyn stares into the rearview. Like an unshakable thought, the black van gets closer. Bolder. Catching up to Hans's limo.

"Victor, what do you mean he's going to kill them?" Marilyn asks, her eyes still on the rearview.

He ignores the question. There's no time. It gets closer, "Hans, how far are we from the shop?"

"Victor!"

"Not far, sir, but I won't be able to lose them." Hans shifts his eyes away from the road for a half second to peer through the mirror. His toad-like eyes blink and turn back to the road, awaiting orders.

"That's fine, Hans." He says, pinching the bridge of his nose, fighting off a headache. "Marilyn, I'm going to need you to do something for me."

She shakes her head, "Not unless you tell me what you meant."

Victor groans, a pang of electricity throbs in his head, "There's no time."

"Yes, there is!"

"Marilyn, please, I'll explain everything, let's just get to Mrs. Hans's shop alive first. Alright?" The pain pulses.

And Hans slows to a stop in a parking spot across the street from the shop.

And Marilyn nods.

"Great. Hans can you get us closer?"

"I'm afraid not, sir, that space is restricted."

"Why?"

"In case of emergency evacuations, I believe, so that there are no cars blocking the exit."

"Victor," Marilyn interrupts, "What is it you need me to do?"

And the pain pulses. And he thinks of the yellowish liquid in its tube, on the windowsill in the little white house in Sawmill.

"We need to deal with our tail."

He walks out of the limo onto the dirty streets. They try to swallow him, but he knows better than to let them see his fear. He lets them feast on his anger and nothing more.

And he can see the black van out of the corner of his eye. The expensive black van. Why would they use a car like that for a chase? Unless it wasn't a chase... But that wouldn't matter if his plan worked. If it doesn't...

He doesn't want to think of what would happen if it doesn't. Because he would be afraid. And the city swallows the afraid.

The city is loud even at this hour. People are crowding the

streets, driving or walking to Wren's citadel. All dressed for a party. Whereas he looks like he's been run over by a train and survived.

He can see his tail walking out after him. Wolff has always had his opinion of tails, people sent out to follow other people. He sees them as creeps. But at the moment, the guy following him looks like a different type of creep. Ordinary guy, not too built with black glasses and a beige suit. The very definition of a plainclothesman. Which stands out a little too much in a place like Urbis.

Victor steps onto the sidewalk and into the bank. There's a snaky line of people waiting on the human bankers, but Victor turns to the abandoned automated tellers lining the farther walls. His wallet is stuffed with good old untraceable cash, useless in day-to-day transactions and regular deals. But Wren hasn't had many of those, "regular deals".

He draws out some money, enough to buy time. He can still see his creep in the reflection of the machine, waiting right outside the door as if he's talking on the pay phone at the entrance. But his lips hardly move.

He turns and the man keeps talking.

Victor walks into a hotel next door to the bank. The wash of golden light bleaches him.

"Welcome to the Utopia Hotel by Norton Crow, how may I help you?"

The pain pulses again, stronger. Victor hides his pain behind a smile and a small stack of good old fashioned cash. "Hey, I need you to do something for me. You see these?"

"Yes, sir, you can pay your stay electronically."

"I can pay the hotel electronically, if that's what I wanted to do. Which is what I want a man in a beige suit to think is what

I'm doing." He slides the bills onto the desk, looking into the shiny golden column behind the receptionist to catch sight of his tail.

"I'm sorry, sir, I–I'm not sure I understand."

"Tell him I'm in room '49 on the top floor. Make it believable. Please, this man is following me."

"Should I call the police?"

The pain sends a sting through his head. "No, no police. Look, I'm paying you directly, this can't affect the hotel in any way, just send him to an empty room. Stall him as long as possible. Can you do that for me?"

"Um—"

Victor slides a couple more bills.

Her eyes don't light up. But she sees him, the man in a beige suit.

"Okay."

"Great, thank you." He leaves the receptionist, risking a final look back to make sure his tail is just gonna be bold enough to follow him into the elevator. Fortunately, the man stops at the front desk. But another plainclothesman is heading directly toward the elevator, eyes shifting at Victor a little too often.

* * *

"Here, put these on."

The concierge hesitantly puts on a black jacket, ripped at the shoulder. "I'm not sure I should be doing this."

"You'll be fine." Marilyn reassures him. She looks out the window into the light of a thousand skyscrapers.

"I could get fired for this, is all I'm saying."

She looks back at him. He's already changed into the clothes she had left for him. The room is empty. And dark. Very dark. There's two beds and a huge window with canvas curtains.

"You won't get fired." She tells him, even though he's not really fighting it.

The concierge walks over to her. Marilyn watches his hands, fidgeting and sweaty, as he stops in front of the bed where his uniform is folded.

"This is risking a lot," he says, "I think I need some kind of guarantee that I won't get fired."

She turns away from the concierge and looks out the window. But she's not looking at the buildings or the streets.

"You have a guarantee."

"How?"

She watches the sky, standing still but it looks like it's moving.

"I'm Marilyn Crow."

* * *

The sweaty palms and beaded forehead. The shifting eyes and the pricked up ears. The cold stare into the distance. Victor knows a tail when he sees one.

He practically slams the "Close Doors" buttons, but they're just as useful as ever, and the man barges in just before the doors slide shut.

"Almost missed it." Victor laughs.

The man just grunts, staring holes into the door.

"What floor are you going to?"

The man hesitates, "Uh—Four."

"Really? I was just going down."

"Down?" The man turns sharply, but Victor is already swinging a punch at his jaw. He feels the momentary weightlessness of the elevator going down.

The tail stumbles back, but he returns with a punch which Victor readily dodges and counters with a blow to the stomach and an elbow to the nose. The plainclothesman flies backwards, sweat spilling through the air. He hits his head against the metal railing and slumps unconscious to the floor.

Victor checks for a pulse.

A beat.

A beat.

He sighs and stands back up.

The doors slide open onto an empty laundry room. Empty except for a gun aimed at his head. And a pulse of pain.

"Oh, you made it." Marilyn lets out the breath she was holding. He can see the fear gripping her hands. He can almost see the connection between her and the gun, and how badly she wants to let go of it.

"Ouch."

"I heard punches, I thought he might have caught you."

"And beat me up? They—could you put that gun down, you're making me nervous, thank you—they should know better than that."

"I can see that."

"I meant to take him awake." He feels the need to reassure her.

She holds her breath again. "Is he—"

And he can't explain it. But he hears *um*. And he hears a promise. *I'm not like him.*

"He's alive."

She nods. "Okay."

"But we should probably put him somewhere more comfortable."

"How's premium linen?" She says, pushing a cart out of the way of the ramp.

They lift the unconscious man into a cart with bleach-white linen bedding and push it behind a washing machine. The cycle spins, sending white sheets splattering against the door. Victor sees his own reflection in the water droplets left dripping down.

He can't decide what he sees.

He sees himself. And someone else, a stranger in his own skin.

He shakes it off. Time's running out.

"Where's the loading dock?"

Marilyn leads him up the ramp to the back side of the building. And they can only hope their tail is somewhere at the top of the building in room '49 and not behind them, running.

Running like them.

Running into Mrs. Hans's shop. Where she greets them with a smile.

Her hair is jet black to contrast her husband's sliver-white. She's a tall woman of a certain age, and she smiles with her eyes.

"Please, have a seat." She says.

She offers them tea, but the tea is bitter.

Mrs. Hans observes them from behind the smoke of her bitter tea. "You two look very nice together."

Um...

Marilyn laughs, "Is it the grime?"

And Mrs. Hans laughs with her eyes, and she wipes a tear from her eye, "Yes, that might be it. Never mind, we'll fix you. You'll look perfect."

"Thank you, Mrs. Hans."

"Trust me, it's my pleasure. Hans, dear, pass me my keys, we need the real thing."

Hans comes back with the keys. She clicks them into a closet and pulls out a tailored tuxedo and a white jumper. "Hans, can you help me with the boy, I'll handle Miss Marilyn."
Victor takes the longest shower he can afford. Hans himself does Victor's hair, with a few... modern touches of his own. And he looks him dead in the eye.

"Very sharp, Mr. Wolff."

"Thanks, Hans, but you can call me Victor." He realizes it's the first time he's ever said it, and he can't imagine why.

"Thank you, sir."

"You've been at this for a while, haven't you?"

"Yes, sir. Too long." His eyes become solemn. "I've been meaning to talk to you about that. I believe it is time that I retire."

The words bring a bittersweet nostalgia. "Retire?"

"Yes, sir. To spend more time with my daughter and her son. My grandson... He needs me, and I think it's time I dedicated myself to my family."

Victor feels a pressure in his throat, "That's... That's good, Hans. I think you deserve it."

"It's probably something I should have done long ago."

Victor nods. And there's a moment of silence between them.

Until Hans sighs and goes on, "Can I offer you some advice, sir?"

"Of course."

And the air is sucked out of the room. And the mirror looks back at him, and Hans looks back at him. "Men like Adolf Wren are powerful for a reason. They are devilishly clever and have years of accumulated resources on their side. I know you are a devilishly clever young man, Mr. Wolff, and no doubt you will have no trouble acquiring many resources yourself. But there seems to be a path forged for you, written in stone. But there is no stone, sir, that's for you to decide. Don't fall into the holes they have dug for you."

The room seems darker. Victor can feel his hands clenching. He looks down at his shoes. And what scares him is how clearly he can visualize it. Himself in Wren's seat. And the blood around it.

"Wren has broken many things... So have you."

"What am I supposed to do?" His heart thumps behind a rising chest. Thumps faster. Because his teeth are gritted and his blood is freezing over. He feels cold.

"What will you do when you this is over?"

"I don't know."

"Will you fix what you have broken?"

"I don't know if I can."

"But the time will come when you must make that choice. This must happen."

Victor's teeth grit. And he doesn't answer. He feels the weight of the words, balancing on a needle, and the slightest whisper will send it falling. Falling.

This must happen.

"And may I say, sir," Hans smiles, "It never hurts to have the right person at your side when it does."

* * *

"You've come quite a long way."

Marilyn brings her eyes away from the mirror. "What?"

"You and Victor, you've come all this way." Mrs. Hans is smiling, but there's something else. A different gleam in her eyes.

"Oh, yes." She tries to smile back, but her eyes are on the mirror. She still feels the string tying her to that trigger. The trigger beside her. And the gun.

"You're concerned."

The lights around the mirror light up her face. She can see her eyes, and she sees a glint in them, like a tear that won't come out.

And she nods because she can't say it.

And she looks at the gun.

"That thing is a tool, it has no hold over us."

"It's made Victor do horrible things." It emits a darkness, like the pulse of a rotten heart, and the whisper of a cursed tongue. "Made *me* do horrible things."

"You're worried about him."

She nods, and between gulps, she says, "He lies, and he kills. And it comes so easy to him."

And now she's not smiling. Not with her eyes. "You're right to be worried. I'm worried for him too."

Marilyn looks away from the mirror. And she sees a tear slide down Mrs. Hans's face.

"My husband only tells me parts of the stories. But I know how they end. And I worry for him."

"It's like he's wearing a mask I can never see through. I've seen what he's capable of and it scares me."

Mrs Hans doesn't seem to be listening anymore. And she talks to herself, and she cries.

"That boy is more dangerous than anyone gives him credit for. And he's blocked the monster off with layer after layer of lies and justifications he's made for himself. But inside that shell is trauma only he knows."

"I can't let him become like Wren."

"That man turned an innocent boy into his tool. His gun. But he's not lost yet. We mustn't let him get lost."

Marilyn watches the tear shine with the light of the mirror, and she watches it stream down Mrs. Hans's wrinkled cheek. Wrinkled from smiling with her eyes. And dampened by crying with them.

* * *

She's waiting for him, dressed in her white jumper, her hair tied up with a black ribbon.

His words freeze in his mouth.

"You look splendid, madam." Hans voices.

"You do." Victor agrees.

"Thank you. You don't look so bad yourself."

"I'll let you finish getting ready." Mrs. Hans says as she walks out of the room.

Marilyn breaks the silence. "I like her. She's fun."

"Yeah," Victor answers, "Mrs. Hans used to send food for me with Hans sometimes. She's probably saved me from starvation a couple times."

She smiles, but just as soon becomes pensive. "You think we're gonna make it?"

"I think we'll be fine. Wren taught me everything I know. Tonight he's gonna regret it."

But she's already thinking of something else. "What did you mean he's going to kill them all?"

Victor has to take a breath before he answers. "The people

walking into his party... They're all shareholders for the Newton Project. And there's only one way he can get those shares. Negotiate. Unless the shareholders were to have an unfortunate accident."

"So he kills them all? Isn't that a little risky."

"Not if he pushes the blame onto someone else."

"Who?"

"I have some ideas. But it won't matter unless we get that file. And the Source knows we're alive now, they've been tailing us since we got here. They're trying to corner us. Scare us away."

"Why?"

"Because they want Wren dead. And I doubt they mind collateral damage. We have to get that file, get out of there, and save as many people as we can."

Marilyn nods, "Then let's just hope we can get out of this together."

Victor smiles, and Hans interrupts, "Sir, I believe we should be going."

"It won't be long before they find out I'm not on the 49th floor. Did you do what I asked?"

"I bribed the concierge to give them a good chase around the hotel dressed as you. Yes."

And Hans opens the door of the store for them. And Victor opens the door of the limo for Marilyn while Hans starts the engine.

The perfectly quiet hum of the limousine leaves a trail behind them. And they see Mrs. Hans in the rearview mirror. And she's smiling. Smiling with her eyes.

The room was cold. A record played on the turntable behind Mr. Wren's chair.

"It's a gift from an old friend," Mr. Wren said, "Foreign music, I like it, it's new."

"Yes, sir." Victor had answered. He had answered it without thinking.

"Did you do what I asked?"

"Yes, sir. They're both at their apartment, my guess is they should be there for the next couple days at least. They don't have contacts alerted, no police visits, no inquiries. Not yet."

"That's good. Good work, Victor, you're coming along."

"Thank you, sir."

"I believe that's all, you're free to go home or explore the city with friends or whatever it is you teenagers do nowadays."

Mr. Wren had already turned back to his vinyl, but Victor hadn't left. He's finding the words, but there are no words, so he says it as well as he can.

"Mr. Wren, I don't think this is the most logical way."

"Logical, huh? You don't think I should pull the trigger. Alright, why?"

"It's unnecessary dirt, in my opinion."

"Don't ever add 'in my opinion', your words have to be fact, or your argument falls apart. Try again, convince me."

"We'd be drawing unnecessary attention. I'm sure you have your reasons, but we'd just be calling an investigation on us. They might even blame us for Mrs. Crow's death."

Mr. Wren smiled proudly. "Much better. What do you suggest we do?"

"Leave Norton Crow alone, and his daughter."

Mr. Wren crushed a laugh between his teeth. "I can't do that, Victor."

"Then buy him out and give his daughter a job. He can't hurt us without hurting her, and he's not gonna do that. He can't do that."

The record scratched to an end, leaving a repetitive buzz on the speaker. Mr. Wren brushed his hand through his hair. "You really are coming along."

"Thank you, sir."

"Why are you doing it, Victor?"

"Why, sir?"

"Yeah, why are you doing this? Is it pity? Affection?"

"No, sir." Victor felt a knot in his throat.

Mr. Wren's smile vanished and his face became like a stone, "I'm not saying it won't work, it most likely will. But you can't let affections get in the way, Victor, remember that."

"Yes, sir."

"I'm doing this as a favor to you, kid. But this is the last time. And I can't promise to protect her from anything after this."

Victor knew it would stack up to this. He'd expected it. But suddenly it felt more real. "I understand."

And there was a beat before Mr. Wren went on. A beat filled with more meaning than any words could ever manage.

"You're free to go. Take care, Victor. I'm proud of you." He said, flipping the record over and letting it play Side B. Letting it play quietly.

18

"Alright, I think we all know the plan, but let's go over it one more time for the sake of being on the same page."

Mrs. Hans had given them lunch to take with them. Victor and Marilyn sip at the soup, trying to keep it from sloshing around through the turns.

"We're making good time and we've probably lost our tail by now. Let's just hope no stray informant decides to phone Wren before we get to the party."

"Because we're dead." Marilyn says.

"Dead and fired. We can't risk having him on his guard. As far as he knows, this is a victory for him."

"Right." Marilyn puts the lid on her soup. "But what if he sees you at the party."

"If everything goes the way it should, and I'm hoping every-thing goes the way it should, I won't have to be at the party."

"You'll be in his office."

"That's right. Considering the day we've been having, our time frame isn't bad. I slip in, slip out, and we ride off into the sunset. It's a solid plan, relatively."

"Relative to what?" Marilyn says.

"Not important. What's important is that he doesn't see *you*."

"Because the plan blows up if he does."

"Because we blow up if he does."

"And me, sir?" Hans asks.

"You might wanna tell Mrs. Hans to pack her bags, Hans."

"Where are we going?"

"How's a trip to Mar Cresta sound?"

"I love the beach."

"Do we get a trip to the beach?" Marilyn asks.

Victor smiles. "Put this in your ear." He hands her a small earpiece.

She tests it, and asks, "Can you teach me to do that thing you do?"

"What thing?"

"To know what people are thinking."

"Oh. That's easy." He turns to face her. "A person's world is reflected in their eyes. Their thoughts are written all over them, you just have to know how to read them."

"And how do you do that."

"When I'm talking to someone, I always look them in the eye, lies and truths can be hidden by voice, but not through the eyes. When someone is looking into your eyes, you control the conversation, and you control what people think because in that moment, they know that you know their thoughts."

"So people are easy to manipulate."

"Only if they don't know they're being manipulated."

"Can we manipulate Wren?"

He takes a while to answer. Because he doesn't know. And he doesn't know what might happen if he looks into Wren's eyes. Because Wren can read him too. As easy as reading a picture book.

"I don't know."

And the limo drives up to an enormous building in the center of the city. People are lining up on a red carpet, noise flying everywhere, shooting through the wind like darts. A guard noses over a clipboard at the entrance.

"Victor, how are we going to get in?"

"I'm working on it. Come on." Hans keeps the engine running. The light bleeds through the open door. Victor takes a sip of his soup with Marilyn walking at his side. Guards circle the building, tramping down a line of edges around the citadel. Victor walks the same line around the building. A bald guard turns a corner in front of him.

Victor keeps his head down, but he knows the guard's already recognized him. And he throws the soup at the guard's head, taking the momentum to rush at him and knock the gun out of his hand. The guard sends a soup-drenched punch at Victor's head, which Victor dodges and counters with a kick to the side and a punch right into the middle of that shiny bald head. The punch knocks the guard into the wall. He falls in a heap, unconscious. Victor checks his pulse as a surge of adrenaline runs through him.

Still alive. Just unconscious.

Victor sighs to himself. And he realizes, for the briefest moment, he felt fear. Fear that he had killed the guard.

He crouches over the guard. Still alive. Wolff soothes his knuckles. He takes the radio from the guard's belt and listens for his name. But there's nothing.

He clicks the button on the side and the radio crackles with static. "He's here," He says into the radio, "Larousse is coming around the back, don't let him in."

He wipes down the radio and puts it back into the guard's belt. He sits the guard against the wall and flicks a noodle off his forehead, and he wipes a drop of soup off his own shirt.

"Beautiful." He says to himself, looking at the orange stain on his shirt.

The line is stopped, and Marilyn is already mixed in with the crowd. There's no guard.

They push through to the front of the line and into the elevator with a few other people too important to be kept waiting.

"Good evening." A woman of uncertain age dressed in a long purple dress and a matching fedora complete with dark veil which almost completely obscures her face is facing them.

"Good evening," They answer blankly.

"Are you friends of dear Wren."

"Something like that." Victor says.

"That's right, Adolf doesn't have friends, does he?"

"I wouldn't know. Are you shareholders?" Victor is dying for the woman to take off her veil. It bothers him that he can't read her expression, while he's completely uncovered.

And the man beside her is quiet and unreadable, as if he's not listening at all, but blocking it out with a veil of his own.

"What? Oh no, the project is our brainchild, I suppose that's why he invited us. But we haven't seen him in a while."

"Your... brainchild?"

"Oh—The doors." And the doors slide open, and the lady disappears into the white wash of light and music.

A mass band dressed in red and gold is playing passionately, lost in their art.

People talk. They dance. But there's no trace of Wren.

"He must still be in his office." Victor tells Marilyn. "We'll have to mingle for a bit."

"Fun." She replies sarcastically.

18

No one talks to them, and they're already grateful for it. As much as possible, they have to be plain. Forgettable. Unnoticed.

Victor had never been antisocial; it isn't in his nature, but it has to be done. So he does something he learned long ago. One of Wren's first lessons. He dances.

The band dishes out song after song.

"You remember the plan?"

"The one you told me about or are we talking about some other plan you just came up with?"

"I like to improvise."

"You like putting yourself in dangerous situations with no way out."

"I've made it this far."

"Not without almost dying."

"*Almost.*"

"You're going to get yourself killed eventually."

Victor smiles. He'd never thought of it before, but for some reason it doesn't scare him. It seems too distant to fear.

"You need to be more careful."

Careful. He'd never given that much thought either. "What fun would that be?"

Marilyn scoffs. "What happens when we get the file?"

"We get it to Emperor Priev. Egeria is the only planet with some kind of military chance against whatever's on that file."

"What if he won't help us? He already doesn't trust you. What if—"

But suddenly, the music stops, and the dancers stop, and the air is choked out of the room as footsteps fill the silence. Footsteps like toxin. The singer steps away from the microphone. And the voice is like poison. And the eyes are squinted and keen.

"Good evening, I hope you're having fun. Let me raise a toast to my dear friend, Norton Crow, who has unfortunately passed away in a malfunction of his private Nav."

19

Everything is blurry.

Because there he is. Two rows down, standing over the party. Casting a shadow across the room. And something stirs up in Victor that he can't explain. A blur. A smoke. But those words can't quite explain it. Because it's Fear.

And before he can fully realize the thought, Marilyn is charging forward. Victor pulls her back.

If he had been one second too late, their cover would have been blown. And Wren's eyes would have been scratched out. She's seething.

"Calm down." He whispers, but the people's cheers are too loud, and he has to repeat it louder. "Listen, we can't kill him, remember? That's not why we're here."

"Let me go," She growls back at him. "Can't you hear him, he's lying!"

"I know." And he *is* lying. For no reason, he's spitting out an empty lie carelessly. And Wren isn't careless. He's a lot of things, but he's not careless. He wouldn't tell a lie like that without a motive. "I know, but we don't have time for that right now. *Especially* right now."

She scowls.

"We're too close to him." *And he might already know we're*

here.

"Let's go." He walks her over to the bar and gets her a glass of sparkling water. "Keep your head clear." He smiles.

But she doesn't.

And he can't turn around.

But he does, and it takes the weight of all the air in the jazz-music, lie-poisoned, ball-of-killers-thieves-know-it—alls-and-innocent—know-nothings atmosphere to pull him away. To pull him into the shadow of Wren's toasts and the crowd of people who have no idea what's coming or what's already come.

People smile at him with their most convincing fake-happy on. They nod and greet. But he doesn't answer. Some people may recognize him. He doesn't know if any of them would actually rat him out to Wren, but he doesn't doubt it. He just hopes they have that sliver of real-happy left. And none of them can know he's dead or fired anyway.

He feels a tap on the shoulder.

"Victor?"

"No." Victor answers in a half-wince.

"What are you doing here? I didn't think I'd see you."

There's something slightly familiar about him, but Victor can't place it. He's thin, pencil-thin, and there's that better-than-you smirk pasted on his tissue-paper-rubbed face.

And his name is obnoxious.

"Why wouldn't I be, Michel?"

"I just thought you'd quit."

"You need a job, Michel?"

Michel Delune reminds Victor of an ant under a boot, scurrying to fit between the cracks of the sole. He's one of those ants you just can't seem to crush.

"Well, I think I might fit the bill."

Victor can see Marilyn urging him over the rim of her glass to get out of there. Michel catches him looking and turns around. "Who's that?" The smirk stretches his thin lips.

"Let me give you a tip, Michel, you wanna be like me, go home, take a look in the mirror, and find out how you became such a melted birthday candle. Alright? Enjoy the party."

Michel scoffs, but it's clear he's grasping for words. He smirks, but it's just more fake-happy.

Victor walks away, unable to help thinking that the uncrushable ant's next target would be Marilyn, or worse, Wren. He turns to look for him, but he's already lost across the room.

"Marilyn," He calls through the comm, "There's a guy around here somewhere, he saw me."

"What's he look like?" She answers back.

Like a little pampered goldfish who swam too deep for his tiny flippers to handle.

"He's thin, obnoxious, and so full of himself that if he tipped over, he'd spill his life story right on everyone's white shoes."

"...okay."

"You'll know him when you see him."

"I'll handle it, you get the file."

As she says it, the hall ends and he's standing in front of a door. He types in the code, but it blinks red.

And the hits keep on coming. Because there's only one person who is sure to have the code. And he's currently shaking hands and handing out lies, hors d'ouvres, and champagne.

Unless...

He walks back to the elevator. It's abandoned by everyone and everything except the far-away chatter from behind the double doors.

Victor takes a turn into the bathroom and locks himself in a stall. He takes out the radio. He'd turned it off for the sake of the jazz-musicians, but he hears the crackle of it now. And voices.

"Anyone have eyes on the intruder?"

"Is it him?"

"We're not sure."

"Someone get up to Wren, there's nothing down here. He's inside the building."

Victor clears his throat and brings the radio to his mouth. "I have eyes on the intruder."

"Location?"

"He doesn't know I'm onto him."

"Give us your location, we'll send reinforcements."

Victor shuts it off and thinks.

And it crackles again.

And he puts it to his mouth.

Because there's only one other person who might have the codes. But it's a long shot. And he lays the accent on thick.

"Does anyone have Orlan's location?"

"What?"

"I report only to my brother."

"Oh, you're one of them. One of you contact Orlan on channel 3. Standby, Egerian."

There's silence in the stall. Until the door opens. He sees boots walking in front of the stall, and they turn away from him. The water runs, and static crackles.

"Yeah?"

"We have eyes on the intruder. One of your guys has him. Channel 7."

"It's him, uh? You're sure?"

The voice is rough, like the crackling of sand in the wind. Like the scorching sun burning a throat. Or like the suffocating wind adapting windpipes to breath easy in a place like Egeria.

It's a voice Victor knows.

He stands still, clicks his radio off, wincing at the click of the button.

"*It's not confirmed.*"

"Uh-huh. I'll talk to him, go back to work, block off the exits. Get someone on the top floor, uh? We can't take any chances."

And there's the click of a button. But Victor turns his radio back on. He ducks down and passes it into the next stall. He fingers the gun in his pocket and draws it out.

And the voices mix.

"*Where is he?*"

He sees the boots turn, and the stall next door open, and a rush of himself pointing the gun at his head, and Orlan leaning down with the radio in hand, and his hands are up, and he's trying to stand.

"Stay down." Victor pulls the hammer back.

His finger shakes on the trigger. He doesn't feel the same electric surge through his arm, like the pulsing of the gun. But it is pulsing.

Orlan clicks the button on the radio. "Talk, brother, let them all hear you."

"*Orlan?*"

Victor whispers. "Put it down."

"I can't hear you."

"Yes, you can, put it down or I'll shoot, and you know I will."

"You're not a killer anymore, uh? Am I not right?"

"Put your gun down." Victor says, louder.

"What?"

"Put it down!"

"Gun?"

"Orlan, put it down! Don't shoot!" And he fires a shot into the ground. The report blasts sound waves which shake the stalls.

And Victor yells. The static crackles from the radio. And Orlan is covering his ears. Victor kicks the radio away and screams. Screams like he's been shot. And he stops screaming.

"*Orlan?*" The radio rattles.

"*Orlan? Has the intruder been neutralized?*"

And *the intruder* pulls the hammer back again. And the barrel is aimed at Orlan's head.

Victor walks around him to get the radio. He kicks Orlan's stunned self over and picks it up. And he smiles.

"Still think I won't shoot?"

Orlan growls.

"What's the code?" He shakes the gun for good measure.

Orlan hisses, "3327."

Victor holds up the radio. "Tell them it wasn't me." He presses the button.

Orlan hesitates. "It isn't him."

The button clicks again. "Tell them the intruder has been neutralized."

"Intruder neutralized."

Victor clicks the radio off. "Good job."

And a grin spreads across Orlan's face. "How long do you think you have before everyone in the building is chasing you, uh?"

"You think so? I hear the music playing pretty loudly."

"You make a lot of noise, Victor Wolff."

"So I hear."

"I hope Wren doesn't catch you, uh—"

"That makes two of us."

"—Because I want to kill you myself."

And it makes Victor smile. Because that's not anger on Orlan's face. It's fear of a worthy opponent.

"I'll see you then, brother."

And the lights are off. Darkness swallows the bathroom. And he feels more than hears Orlan pounce, but he's already out the door. And in the party. And lost in the fake-happy fog of the crowd.

The receptionist is still there. She's sitting in the same place as she was when he saw her last. With the same sarcastic frown.

Victor sighs and walks in.

"Um, can I help you, Mr. Wolff?" She stands up.

Victor stops in his tracks. "No, I'm just getting something I forgot."

"Well, I can get it for you." She offers, more skeptically than in a spirit of kindness.

"Okay, sure."

"You know what's funny?" She says as she unlocks the door.

"How long it takes to unlock this door?"

"It's funny you're here."

Not good. "I don't hear you laughing."

"Mr. Wren told me specifically that you were not under his service anymore." She turns and flashes a tiny gun aimed straight at Victor's chest.

Victor's hands fly up instinctively. "Come on, you're not gonna shoot me, are you?"

"I don't want to." Her hands are shaking, but her eyes are

trained on the tiny ear at the end of her gun. "Just walk away."

"I can't do that."

A click echos in his ears. His heart stops, but his feet jump and the bullet flies past him. Victor balances himself on the desk and snatches the gun out of her hands before she can aim again. He flips the gun to face her. Her hand extends over the desk, reaching for the button on the other side to trigger an alarm.

And at this point, Victor doesn't know what to expect.

"Get away from the desk." He wishes he could remember her name.

She waits. But she stands up and straightens out her dress defiantly.

The little gun feels foreign in his hands. It's a light little thing, and it fits in the palm of his hands. Like a toy. But it shot a hole in the wall.

"Get in the office." He opens the door and she follows. "Close the door." She obeys. "Sit down." He points to Wren's chair. Again, she does as she's told.

Victor rushes over to the desk. The drawers are all locked, but he kicks in the bottom left one, leaving the lock disfigured. The drawer slides open. It's almost empty. There are a few paper files here and there, but nothing digital. He opens two more with no success.

But there's the last one. And a safe inside of it.

"Open it."

She crouches down and taps in the code.

And it clicks open. Victor reaches in, brushing past a couple more paper files.

But there's nothing. He throws the paper files back in and clicks on his comm. "Marilyn, it's not here."

He grits his teeth and kicks the drawer. Something rattles inside. A glass rattle. Victor reaches back into the darkness of the safe. His fingers wrap around something. And he brings out his hand and looks into the glass.

"*Victor,*" Marilyn whispers through the comm, "*There's a problem here, too.*"

"What is it?" He says absently. Because he's watching the glass.

"*She's here.*"

"Who?"

"*The Source.*"

"Oh." He hears it, but he's watching the glass. And a rush of pain thrashes in his skull, it gnaws at his thoughts. "Wren must have the file on him. Does he know we're here?" He groans.

"*He's about to.*" And the comm clicks off.

The pain pulses through him. And he sees the glass. And the needle glimmers in the light. And the yellowish liquid sloshes around inside the little half vial.

20

And he's talking to someone. The guy looks obnoxious, but the light isn't exactly flattering. Marilyn can see people turning to look at them. She thinks of stepping up to help him, but decides that would just draw more attention.

So she watches.

And she looks at Wren. He doesn't look back, but for a moment she wishes he did. She wishes he'd look back at her and be afraid. Looking at a ghost.

But he doesn't look back.

Her hands curl into fists until her nails are biting into her palms.

LOOK AT ME.

She turns back and Victor is walking away. The other man he's with is walking toward the front. Marilyn leaves her sparkling water dripping on the bar and walks through the party. People spin and dip around her, and she follows the man.

And she hears a voice in her ear along with a background screeching, "*Marilyn, there's a guy around here somewhere, he saw me.*"

She's watching him. And she knows it's him. But she still asks.

"What's he look like?"

And Victor describes the exact portrait of the man in front of her. With a few extra steps.

"...okay." She answers, keeping her voice down.

Victor says something Marilyn doesn't catch because the man is turning around, and she hides behind the crowd.

And she says into the comm, "I'll handle it, you get the file."

And she can feel him looking at her. And she turns around, tapping shoulders as she does.

And he's staring at her, smirking like it's plastered on his face.

"You're with Vic, right?"

"Vic?"

"Victor, you're with him, right?"

Marilyn fake-smiles, "He's with me."

The man laughs, "That sounds about right."

"And you are?"

"I'm sorry, I forgot to introduce myself. I'm Michel Delune."

And his name is obnoxious.

He stretches out a hand for her to shake.

"Marilyn Finch." She says, searching the room without knowing why. "How do you know Victor?"

Delune smiles like he's recalling a memory from a long time ago, and he starts speaking like he's remembering the time he bought an ice cream in the hot sun. "We met a little while back, or actually, we met at a party back when we were applying for the internship with Mr. Wren, but I don't think he remembers that."

"Oh." She finds it's the only correct response.

And the bitterness creeps in. Because he's remembering when another kid stole his ice cream. "But Vic got the internship. Younger, less experienced. He got it because I didn't even get a chance to interview. Because Adolf Wren *liked* him and canceled all other interviews."

"I'm sorry to hear that."

He smiles, but there's still something rancid behind it. "So was I. He got it because he happened to get there first. But you don't have to worry, I'm here to take it back."

"What?" But she's already searching the room again on instinct. Something in her is whispering, screaming, for her to look around and she knows why. Because standing in the corner of the room, glaring knives into her, is a tall, dark woman in silver gloves up to her elbows. And the room stops moving, and an ominous vignette draws itself tightly around her. It's Delune's voice which brings her back, because he's not talking about his childhood disappointments anymore.

"A bit of advice about our friend. Vic Wolff really only looks out for himself. He might act like the savior of the world, but there's really only one skin he's trying to save. And he'll do anything to reach the top." He's no longer making any effort to conceal his bitterness, "There is a beast hiding behind that smile which has no trouble killing to survive."

"What?" She's only hearing half of what he's saying, but it's enough to make her want to get out of this party.

"How do you think he's gotten this far? What kind of work do you think Mr. Wren puts him up to?"

And she knows, but she knows she wishes she didn't.

"Excuse me, Miss Finch, it was nice meeting you." He says, walking away with the trail of bitterness leaving a strange gravity.

And Marilyn lets him go. She forgets where he's going and why he's going. He's walking toward Wren. But how has he gotten this far? How has Victor survived this long?

How far gone are you?

"*Marilyn,*" Victor's voice comes through the comm, "*It's not here.*"

"Victor," She realizes she's still breathing loudly and brings her voice to a more normal volume, "There's a problem here too," Her hands are shaking, she doesn't know if she should tell Victor about Delune, because she can see him from here, and he's already talking to Wren. "She's here." Should she ask him about what Delune said? "The Source."

Then he asks the question, "*Does he know we're here?*"

The comm buzzes in anticipation, waiting for an answer.

"He's about to."

"Miss Finch." A voice half-whispers into her ear. For a moment, Marilyn thinks it's still Victor talking through the comm, but there's no buzzing. And she feels the cold breath of the voice. Marilyn tries to keep a straight face. To keep her dread from leaking out in the space between her lips. And she sees her stern expression, almost like a scolding mother.

The Source.

"I thought we had an agreement."

Marilyn tries to fight down a gulp. "I must have missed that part, was it after you left us to die in a hole?"

"Leave now, before you get yourself hurt." The Source's glare is almost physically painful. There's a power in her eyes, like she's holding your throat in her gloved hand, lightly, so you barely feel it, but you feel it, and you know it can tighten. It can pull your voice from your lungs. And you want to please her, as much as you may hate her, you want to please her. Because she holds your voice.

"We can't let you kill him."

"Do you really think you can stop us?"

"Who is us?" Marilyn says, almost gasping for air.

"Us, The Source, my life's work. My team."

"Victor has an incriminating file on Wren," She says, hoping the lie doesn't show right through her, "We can put an end to this before it starts. *Without* killing him."

"It already has started."

Marilyn stares into The Source's eyes. There's something hiding behind them. She doesn't want to know what it is. But she has to. "What did you do?"

"There's no saving him now."

Marilyn sees the curves of her eyebrows, but she focuses on the shifting of her eyes. But they're not shifting, they're fixed on her.

"No saving him? I don't see a gun to his head."

"In a way, we do have a gun to his head. And it's almost ready to shoot. But I'm giving you one last chance to get out of here, Marilyn Crow."

And the shift happens. Her eyes. For a split second, her eyes shift to the ceiling.

Marilyn swallows, she feels the very intentional prick of The Source's words. Her name. But the shifting. She doesn't know what to ask. She thinks of Victor. Thinks of what he would say, but nothing comes to her. Nothing except sarcastic comments and direct questions like, "What are you planning?" Or "How are you gonna kill him?" Or "Have you tried meditation?" Which makes her think of what Victor would say. And nothing comes to her.

"What's the matter, Miss Crow?" The Source gives her a cruel half-smirk, something barely detectable except in her eyes, which Marilyn stares at intently, trying to disguise it.

"Have you finally come to your senses and realized Wren *must* die?"

But then she stops thinking of what Victor would do. Because she's not Victor. And she doesn't like talking.

"Wren is already tied to the rails, Miss Crow, and I can hear the train coming. I think you're going to miss it."

And her eyes shift up again.

And Marilyn doesn't talk.

What's on the roof?

She smiles.

And The Source's smirk vanishes like a smear of grease wiped off a windshield, and a world-crushing anger smears over her green eyes. "Where is Wolff?"

But she just smiles.

And she sees something she never thought she'd see in The Source's eyes. Fear. A good, generous smear of fear. And now she talks, "Wherever he is, I hope he brought a coat. It's awfully windy outside."

"Where is he?" The Source sneers.

A shiver runs down Marilyn's spine as she watches The Source grasping for words.

"You'll never get to Wren in time to save him. In the end, it is going to come down to saving Wren or saving everyone else."

The words are out. And Marilyn connects the dots. She tries to decide whether she should keep up the lie, or spill her thoughts. But the lie wins over, wins with a smile showing her teeth, "He's got the bomb, all he has to do is throw it off the roof."

"You'll just kill more people."

"And what about all these people? They're just supposed to die because of Wren?"

"There's nothing else to be done. They're *all* too dangerous to be left alive."

"That's not your call to make." She can feel fear trying to climb out. She pushes it back down.

"That's enough," The Source scolds, "You're going to tell Wolff to leave the bomb on the roof and get out of our way."

The finality of the command is evident. The Source is angry, and this is a woman whose anger can burn plains. And she wouldn't hesitate to kill one more person. Marilyn looks around for a way out. She pretends to touch her earpiece, "Victor," a journalist is interviewing people and coming her way, and a waiter with a tray of drinks, "Forget the bomb, we have to get out of here."

The drinks fly through the air because Marilyn whips around and comes crashing into the waiter. The Source flinches and reaches out. And it takes only that split second for Marilyn to slip away.

She grabs the journalist by the arm as she passes. The journalist almost trips backward from Marilyn dragging her away.

"You see that woman over there?" Marilyn points at The Source.

"Yes." The columnist is clearly shaken, but she's already jotting down in her notebook.

"She's got inside information on Adolf Wren's transports."

"She what?" A brand new light comes into her eyes, like someone who's woken up from a dream and steps into a cold shower.

"She's got some kind of document with deals and trades. All sorts of things." The Source has recovered from the punch to her ego and is whipping her head around like an owl.

"Wait, what's her name?" But the journalist is already on her own. Marilyn can hear her asking again, and she sees her straightening her hair and trying to get The Source to talk, but she's not listening, she's looking for Marilyn with her catlike eyes until a flash of light from a camera blinds her long enough for Marilyn to mix in with the crowd. She slides into a corridor. People slither by, dancing or talking. They sound to her like vipers sticking out their forked tongues and searching the air for her scent.

She breathes in, tapping the comm in her ear. She can hear the wasp-like buzzing of as it opens its arms to welcome her voice.

"Victor," She says through the feedback, "We need to get to the roof now."

But there's no answer.

"Victor!" She repeats in a whisper-scream, "We need to get to the roof now!"

She takes her hand from her ear. She can feel a glaze of fear coming over her, clenching her stomach. There's a sting to hearing nothing but the buzz of the wasps. And it hits its mark.

Her knees buckle from under her and a shower of dread washes her over. Her breath shakes, but she breathes in.

"Okay," She steadies herself. Her mind shuffles through all the possibilities, but she stops herself and focuses on the facts. She can't help Victor. And she brings herself to face it.

If he's...dead, she thinks, *then going for him would be good for nothing. But if he's alive, then the bomb will just kill everyone anyway.*

She straightens herself up and breathes away the dread. *No time to be overwhelmed.*

And she walks out of the corridor, struggling the first few

steps to keep herself up, but as she walks out into the snake pit, she remembers something else Victor had taught her. He'd taught her without even realizing it. As she walks toward the stairs avoiding Wren's eyes, she mutters under her breath, breathing to steady herself.

And she mutters:

"Never let them see your fear."

21

Victor slams the drawer shut while the receptionist watches him with a steely-eyed frown. The hatred radiates off her venomous glare. He can't remember her name, except for the fact that it ends with Ana.

And Ana won't listen to a gun, so he shoves it in his pocket.

"We have to get out of here." He says.

"No! We're staying here!"

"Listen, Ana," She makes a face which he chooses to ignore, "If I don't get out of here, I'm dead, you're dead, we're all dead. Look around, you're an accomplice now."

"You made me do it!"

"You think that's gonna matter to Wren?"

She swallows. The words push their way through her stubbornness. "Fine."

"Good, come on." Victor opens the door, positioning himself behind it in case Orlan's welcoming party is early.

But the room is empty, to Ana's visible disappointment. She'd never liked him, and he'd liked her just about enough to not remember her name.

Victor pushes past her, gun drawn and primed, to open the next door.

The door slides open and he hears the clicking of the gun

203

before he sees the barrel staring between his eyes. He can almost see the bullet just aching to bury itself in the furthest corners of his brain.

And he can hear Ana sigh behind him. He can't tell if she's relieved or scared. Or both.

"Three steps back and put the gun down." The mouth behind the gun mutters, his teeth biting down on every word.

"Does everyone want me dead?" Victor laughs. He laughs but he obeys. He's humbled by the gun to the head and leveraged by the bullet inside it. But that's not the only bullet in the room, is it?

He takes another step back as a test. And he steps back forward. And he's still alive. Three more guards block the doorway, aiming their guns at Victor's chest.

Because if one to the head doesn't kill him, three to the chest might do the trick.

It's flattering. The odds of having four against one make him smile.

"Two more," The guard says.

And he's shaken. The fear is written all over his face like permanent ink.

Victor takes a step back. And the second step is a crease in the carpet. The half-second of free-fall passes in slow-motion, and it gives him enough time to trace the path of the bullet.

The guard flinches to catch him, and Victor pulls back the trigger as his back hits the floor. The bullet slices through the air and into the guard's shoulder.

And Ana screams.

And the guard doesn't even have time to scream before Victor's foot slams into his jaw which sends him flying back into the other guards.

Victor hides behind the guard's burly hunched over body. His bullish human shield reaches over to try to grab him, but Victor sends a punch into his spine which makes him shudder.

Wolff slides his hand under the recovering guard's arm and sends a volley of bullets through the door, not even taking the trouble to aim.

He's not shooting to kill, but it gets them out of the way.

He has to hit one or two of them in the leg, but they get the message.

And his human shield closes his arm around Victor's hand. The gun starts to slip, he can feel the pressure on his wrist making his grip loosen. He aims a kick at the back of the guard's knee, but he misses, because the guard loses his balance, and he's falling forward. He lands with closed eyes, as a small puddle of blood forms around his shoulder.

Victor takes aim, but the guard's eyes are closed. His head is leaning onto the ground. Victor almost leans down to check his pulse, and a flush of fear runs through him. But he hears the pulse of hammers pulling back and guns aimed at him from behind the doorway.

The fear is written all over their faces. And they won't shoot. They're staring at the gun in his hand. It feels lighter to him. And it's warm.

"Get behind me." He whispers to Ana.

The guards are hiding behind the walls, and they can't shoot him unless he crosses that door. And then it's roulette because they know they won't all make it. So they wait.

And Victor's gun is trained on the door. He takes a few steps forward, but the guards don't show their teeth.

"You're not gonna kill them, are you?" Ana whispers back. Her voice is shaking now.

"Shh."

"You can't shoot them."

"I'm not gonna shoot them." He says. And relief drains from her. "You are."

"What! No, I can't! I won't!"

"You can, you will." He pulls the tiny gun out of his pocket and reaches his hand out. She takes it hesitantly as he begins to push her toward the door.

"Don't shoot!" She yells.

"They're not gonna shoot you," Victor tells her, "I promise, you'll be alright, but they will if they think I'm coming out first. You have to lead." He doesn't know why he's explaining it to her. But he can see the genuine fear on her face. Like permanent ink.

And he sees her breathing slow down the slightest bit. He has his gun drawn, and it pulses through his arm, but the trigger feels more rigid.

The cold air in the room makes the hairs on his arms stand up. And Ana crosses the room, breathing in heavily that stale air. Victor can't ignore the adrenaline pumping with every heartbeat. But he doesn't hesitate. There's no time for that.

Ana looks back at him with doe-eyes. Victor gives her a reassuring nod. But he can see her eyes looking for a way out. So he whispers to her, "It's alright, they won't hurt you. You'll be alright, just keep your head up. Don't let them see your fear."

She nods back and keeps walking. She crosses the threshold, and a tear drips from her eyes as she turns to get every guard at the tip of her mini-pistol.

He dreads the sound of gunfire, but Ana doesn't seem the type that'll let herself be shot down without taking a couple guards with her.

"Put your guns down!" Victor yells from inside the room.

He hears the rattle of guns as they lower. Lower, he hopes. The board is set. The crossfire is his no man's land, and it's his move.

He takes a breath and steps out in front of her, aiming at the guards. She turns her back to him, brandishing her own gun.

Victor leads her past the guards. They're furious, he can tell from the tension bleeding from their eyes. And they're scared.

And they're letting him pass. Him and Ana, who holds her place in front of him, protecting him from the guards' dangerous instincts.

"Go back to Wren," He tells the guards, "There's someone here who'll try to kidnap him, that's why I'm here, just leave them to me. Tell him you found me, and that I'm dead. It'll buy me some time. And then I'll leave. Win-win."

There's a moment of quiet. The guards seem to be calculating what the collateral would cost them. Then one of them starts for the stairs. And the other follows. The last one steps up to Victor. "You catch your target, and you leave. Then you don't show your face again."

"Yes, sir." Victor answers. Because there's a strange pitch in the guard's voice. Like fear, but calculated fear.

And the guard walks off, leaving them behind. Leaving them as if they were dead.

And they're free. Down the hall and away from the room. And the blessed adrenaline drains out of him.

"Good, now all—"

But she's aiming the gun at him, and glaring.

"You would have made me shoot them."

"I told you you wouldn't have to."

Tears are dripping from her eyes, and Victor feels the false wind of what's to come breathing on him.

And Ana pulls back the trigger.

And she cries, sobbing the guilt away before she can realize the silence in the room. Interrupted by a simple click. The silence of nothing happening.

Victor looks down the barrel of the gun, and he's disappointed. He feels the weight of the bullets in his pocket.

"You should get out of here while you still can."

"What?" Her tears are still flowing.

"Evacuate the building, take as many people with you as you can—"

"What are you talking about? Evacuate?"

"And I'm sorry. You did good. I'm sorry."

Her eyes soften and her tears stop. She nods slightly, because she realizes he's not mocking her. And the gun slides out of her hands.

Victor sees it drop. And he turns around and walks away, making for the stairs, as a shrill whisper buzzes in his ear. And it rises to a shrill scream bursting through his skull. The deafening noise makes him freeze. He presses his head between his hands and almost falls on his back, but he grabs the rail to keep himself steady. Ana is walking toward him, but he doesn't want to think what she'll do. He can't. The sound crowds his brain, screaming at him like a harpy. He gets the urge to tear his hair off and scratch the noise out. He doesn't notice when he falls, just feels the cold floor beneath him, sending shivers up his spine and an icy coolness at the back of his neck making his hairs stand on edge, like they're drawn to finding the source of the noise.

Then the noise dies out. It fades away. And it pulls him out of himself. He feels his pulse slowing down. All he can do is see a blot of Ana scramble to the floor. He doesn't see the gun where she had dropped it.

She's asking him what's wrong. Asking what to do. And her voice is shaking.

He tries to answer, but his lungs won't make the sound, and his lips are stuck together, and there's an intense pain stinging in his head like a magnified migraine. He hears Ana running away from him.

He feels something wrap around his lungs and squeeze, and all the air floods out of him silently. And he feels a burst and there's an empty breathing. He inhales, but there's no way for him to let it out.

And a buzz rings in his ear. And there's another whisper from the harpy hiding in the caves of his skull. But it's the whisper of a familiar voice.

"*Victor,*" her voice sounds urgent and distant. "*We need to get to the roof now.*"

He barely hears it behind the pain drowning it out.

And there's a pause. She's waiting for him to answer. He tries. He tries so hard to form the words, but there's no breath.

"*Victor! We need to get to the roof, now!*"

Victor fights the paralysis and fights to scream, for the comm to catch some sound, but there's no breath. Everything in him is screaming, yelling, pounding inside him, but there's only silence, and the silent struggle of his own anger. And uselessness. And fear. Until the comm stops buzzing, and he's left to his own helplessness.

And he doesn't know if he'll die, but he tries to breathe. It's the closest thing to control he has. Breathing.

He hears footsteps running back toward him. He makes out the blot of someone running. He feels a pill slide through his lips and down his throat. And there's an empty bottle of pills in her hand. Then he feels a strong, bitter smell fill his nose and refresh his lungs. The pill forces itself through him and the fog in his eyes disperses. And he sees Ana watching him blink.

He feels the air fill him and exhales. And he feels the suffocation lifting.

"Thank you." He mutters through his recovering lips.

She nods and smiles slightly.

"I need to get to the roof."

And her smile disappears. "What's on the roof?"

"I don't know. Nothing good. But you should get out of here now."

Ana nods again and helps him up. He feels the strength returning to his legs, but the room still spins.

He steadies himself on the rail and starts climbing. He sees Ana go back into Wren's office. He waits for her, but she doesn't come back, and he's running out of time, he can feel it. And she doesn't come back.

He takes a last look, but it's more of the same. And he climbs. He races up the stairs, and into the fire escape. He doesn't see Marilyn on the way up, but she might already be on the roof.

And he hears running above him on the top staircase. He runs faster, pushes through the door at the top of the fire escape.

The wind almost sends him flying back down the stairs, like a vacuum trying to suck him in. He sees Marilyn just walking out onto the rooftop. He smiles, but she doesn't look back. Because there's four men standing in front of them in armors that look like military stealth outfits, and their handguns are aimed straight at them.

The wind roars through the night, and there's nothing but the floor beneath their feet to keep them on balance. But the soldiers have the same problem.

"Who are they?" Victor asks Marilyn.

"The Source." She answers.

"What are they doing up here?"

"Guarding a bomb."

The words almost knock Victor off balance. "What?"

The soldiers move forward. A black rope is clamped to each one's back, snaking its way to the edge of the roof, where they connect to four small machines.

"Seismic?"

"It'll bring the whole building down floor by floor." She says.

Victor waits, breathing heavily. Two of the soldiers stop a few yards away, while the others keep walking until they're an arm's length away.

And no one makes the first move, because it means leaving themselves vulnerable to the wind.

"None of us want to die." Victor tries to reason, "And one of us has a bomb attached to our chest."

But the soldiers don't answer. And it's clear they're willing to die, as long as that bomb goes off when and where they want.

So Victor does something dumb.

But Marilyn beats him to the punch and drives her knee into the closer soldier's stomach, but it's the wind that takes the kick further.

Victor pushes the other soldier's gun away from his face and throws a punch at his jaw. And he brings his gun to the man's temple. He feels a bullet whistle past him, and sees the other guards taking aim.

Marilyn has her soldier's gun trained on the others.

Their guns are aimed but they can't get a clean shot without shooting their colleagues.

Victor takes the chance to fire a round at one of the soldiers' bulletproof vest. The soldiers flinch out of the way, and the wind fights against them. He pushes his guard off to the side. And he runs.

His legs race against the wind. The soldier punches at him, but Wolff dodges and lands a kick to the vest. The wind carries the soldier to the edge of the roof. The other soldier is already firing at him and radioing for reinforcements. But the wind saves Victor from getting shot, knocking him to the ground. And a bullet crashes into the soldier's vest, and the gunshots stop.

Marilyn is holding her gun steady.

Victor sees the little grappling machine whirring and two more black ropes coiling into it over the side of the building.

"We don't have time," He says as Marilyn knocks the handle of her handgun into the last soldier's head. "Where's the bomb?"

"It has to be on one of them." She yells.

Victor searches through the soldiers, keeping them pinned and tossing their guns over the edge. "What was their plan? Plant the bomb and jump? It's a seismic bomb, they'd die anyway."

"I know that," Marilyn replies harshly. There's nothing on her two soldiers either.

"It's not here!" The ropes coil slower. "It's on one of them."

"What?"

"These were a decoy. The real bomb is on its way up, it's one of them."

Then the machine clicks. Two more soldiers hoist themselves

up onto the roof. Victor fires two rounds to scare them.

And the soldiers run at them.

"Get back down there! One of these will have the bomb."

She's searching one of the downed soldiers for weapons, but she sees the two backups and runs for the fire escape. Victor kicks one of the soldiers in the stomach and throws a punch at the other one. He tumbles onto the first. The soldier lands a punch at Victor's cheek.

No bomb.

He throws himself at the other soldier, but the man dodges and kicks him in the stomach. Wolff rolls and struggles to his feet as the wind blows into his ears. The soldier kicks him harder. And they're on the edge. He can feel the pressure pressing down on him, and gravity taunting him to look over. The soldier gives him a mocking moment to stand before launching another punch.

Victor feels the warmth of something running down the side of his mouth. And he tastes the warmth of bitter iron, runs his tongue over a crack in his lower lip.

The soldier smiles.

Victor spits the blood out beside him and makes an effort to stand up. The soldier draws his fist back for another hit.

And it comes.

Victor blocks the fist. He tumbles himself into the soldier. The man flails his arms to steady himself.

And Victor runs and throws himself, holding tightly to the soldier's torso.

And the wind surrounds them, and wraps them around.

And they fly off the roof, spinning into a whirlwind of free fall.

22

The wind burns at his eyes. And the soldier claws at his hands to get him off. Off to a fall of who knows how many stories, but he can see the blurry little dots of cars speeding by below, and the foamy humidity of the clouds sending stinging raindrops flying onto his face.

He imagines the feeling of falling. The vertigo of the sky surrounding you, suffocating you until you crash to the ground, sending the last shards of your life scattered on the floor in a wash of cracks like glass.

And the height is intoxicating, and the cold is penetrating. So much so that he can feel his hands going numb and his grip faltering. Victor shakes his head to keep his eyes open and launches a blunt punch into his human lifesaver's stomach. But his fist is weak and all he feels is the dullness of the pain in his hand. He cocks his fist back, ready to knock out a few teeth when the line pulls taut.

His hand pulls away and they spin swinging toward the building.

The glass shatters against the soldier's back. Victor feels the impact in his core, and the glass falls like frozen raindrops around him. He winces from the glass splinters gnawing like tiny teeth on his face. Warm drops of blood run down the side of his head. Then comes the second impact of the floor.

Victor brushes a hand softly over his eyes, clearing them of the shards.

And before he sees him he can sense him.

Wren is at the other corner of the room, lording over the chaos like an owl staring down a den of mice, waiting to fly down and slice through their party.

Victor searches the room. Partygoers watch motionlessly, struck dumb by the intrusion. The silence is overwhelming. But he doesn't see Marilyn.

And Wren opens his mouth to speak. But he won't let him talk. He won't let one more word come out of his mouth. He fires a round into the roof. Immediately, the guests down their drinks and the room becomes a coop of over-pampered headless chickens.

But Wren stands still among them all.

The blast had sent a ringing through Victor's ears, but he doesn't mind. He sits among the shards of glass, listening to it crackle under the kicking, shuffling feet of the rushing scared partygoers. He sits down to wait.

"You happy?" Wren asks.

"You can't imagine."

"After all I've done for you."

Victor stands up, holding his finger on the trigger. If he had to shoot he wouldn't hesitate. He wouldn't.

"Haven't I taught you well?"

"To kill?"

"To be a wolf among sheep."

"I don't care. I'm done killing."

Wren grins and laughs in his throat, "No, you're not."

Victor restrains himself from snarling.

"I feel sorry for you, Victor. You could've been great. One of the kings. But I've got more firepower." Wren lifts a gun, Victor hadn't even noticed him draw it. But it doesn't surprise him. A gun to his face is nothing new.

Victor lifts his in turn, but Wren's guards form a circle around him, guns aimed. The guests yell at Wren not to do it. Victor lifts his hands. There's nothing more he can do.

"Good, Victor." Wren taunts.

Victor breathes out. "Aren't you glad you were able to evacuate all these people?"

"They're not out yet."

"Neither are you."

"Aim." Wren shakes his gun. His security guards obey in synchrony. Orlan is at their head, snarling.

Victor fights to keep his eyes open. He wants to see the moment he dies.

The moment they all die.

"I think you'll find that bomb is going off a little earlier than you expected."

Wren looks at Orlan. Orlan turns the guard over. There's a box strapped to his chest. and a panel inside with flashing LED numbers on it in red.

"Twelve minutes." Orlan says. "They were going to crumble the roof on top of our heads."

"That's probably right," Victor says, "That's not how I would've done it."

"Who did this?"

"I'll call you."

"You won't get the chance," Wren says, and the rattle of guns fills the room. "Fi—"

The word gets caught in his mouth as a little can rolls into the room, stopping just in front of Victor.

The entire room turns to look at the little canister. And a thin line of smoke curls up from the tip. Victor fights down the urge to smile and turns one last look at Wren. And chaos erupts.

The canister explodes into a cloud of fog. Victor jumps and breaks into a run as gunfire thrums steadily behind him. He has to squint through the smoke, but his feet don't stop, they carry him, almost floating through the cloud. Before he can register his position, his gun is aimed.

The guards fire aimlessly, blindly. But they're shooting the wrong way.

And his gun is against the back of Wren's head.

"You can't kill me." Wren's voice is calm as ever.

"Give me one good reason."

"Because you're done with killing." His tone seems completely serious, but Victor can imagine the smile behind the words. It makes him want to throw up. He pushes his ego down and smiles.

"I guess you're right." Victor pats him down. And he reaches into Wren's pocket and pulls out a small hard drive with a thin cord snaking behind it. "But I've never been so good at keeping my promises."

And he hears Wren wince. He feels the pushback in his fingers. The resistance as the liquid leaks out into Wren's bloodstream. As the needle breaks through the fabric of his suit. And Wren's body loosens.

"Over here." Victor says. And the gunfire immediately stops. Quiet steps creak toward him.

He keeps his gun to Wren's back and backs up toward the stairway door.

"I'm proud of you, Victor." Wren says, his mind clearly

starting to drift. He says it through gritted teeth, fighting back the pain that must be flooding through his veins

"I don't need you to be proud of me."

"But you have no idea what you've done." It doesn't seem to be a mask. Wren seems almost at ease. "Who's trying to kill me, Victor?"

The question is unsettling.

But Victor closes the door and shoots off running down the stairs. He leaves Wren lying inside the room. Lying. He hears the guards at the top of the stairs carrying Wren. And he hears them running after him. Victor practically slides down the stairs, he can hear bullets hitting the steps behind him, but they're getting too close for comfort.

He breaks through the door which leads him to a bigger hallway with a window at the end and two sets of elevators at the sides. He walks past them and hides his gun. He follows the rest of the running guests and searches them down the main stairs. But none of them are Marilyn. The guards are searching the people a few rows behind, but there's too much chaos and they can't get to all of them.

Victor keeps his head down. And an arm wraps around his.

"What are you doing?" She asks.

The sight of Marilyn sends a shot of relief through him as he answers, "Improvising."

"Hans is waiting outside." She starts walking toward the door.

"There'll be more of them waiting down there."

And there is. Tons. All of them lying outstretched on the floor, being trampled by the escaping partygoers.

"What happened?" Marilyn asks through the noise and screams.

"The Source."

The breeze pushes through the doors and blows against them as they walk out, and then it's still. A warmth of streetlight glows over them. And there's a black limo in the distance.

The guards are catching up behind them. Victor follows Marilyn into the back seat.

The limousine feels oddly unfitting for everything happening outside. People are running around it like a stream rushing around a rock. But inside the limousine everything feels eerily calm.

And then it happens.

There's a roar of flame followed by a shrill ringing. And there's smoke everywhere. A scream and an explosion. And all the lights go out as the building plunges into darkness. And Wren's citadel crumbles in on itself. But there's no sound to it anymore. Just the ringing. And people run faster, their faces caked black with smoke.

And he can't help wondering. Wren is dead. And other cars are coming too.

"Go, that's them." He tells Hans.

Hans starts driving, and the jumping of the limo sends a slight stabbing through Victor's side. He puts his hand in his pocket and takes out the little half-capsule of yellowish liquid, still inside the syringe. Except there's no yellowish liquid inside it anymore. There's only remnant drops of it.

A parade of black trucks grinds past the people from the far side of the building.

Victor opens the window the slightest bit and throws the syringe out. And a painful rush crashes through his skull, and the harpy's screams burst through.

And it vanishes as suddenly as it had started.

And the thought comes to him.
Wren is dead.
And Hans speeds up.

23

The sidewalks are lined with blurs of people as Hans speeds down the street trying to shake the tail of trucks trailing behind them.

"Get down," Victor checks his gun and loads it. A volley of bullets flies past the limousine, crashing into the windows and stopping in the tiny dents they make in the bulletproof glass. Victor clicks the button on the side of the door. He can't resist popping his ears from the change of pressure. He takes a breath and slides out the window, aiming for the wheels.

The wind carries the shots off target. Victor groans and he makes an effort to steady himself against the roof of the car, but Hans's sharp turns make him slide off.

A bullet flies by his ear. Victor instinctively ducks, hitting his head against the roof of the limo. Rubbing his forehead, he lowers himself back into the car. He finds Marilyn loading a gun.

"Where'd you get that?"

"Off one of the guys on the roof, same as that smoke can."

"There's no clean shot, the car moves too much."

Marilyn slides her head out the window and fires two rounds. The last bullet traces a graceful line through the air and bursts the front left tire of the truck directly behind them. The car swerves and stops just off the street, hitting a lamppost.

"I got one!" Marilyn yells from out the window.

"Mhm." Victor says through the lump of pride in his throat, "Good job."

"We're almost there." Hans announces just as another bullet finally shatters the rear window.

Tiny shards of glass fly all over the leather seats, falling like rain on top of Victor and Marilyn.

"Keep your head down." Marilyn says.

Victor shakes off the glass and cocks his gun again. He only has a few rounds left, but he has a feeling it's his last chance to shoot.

Now or never.

He braces himself, trying to calculate the interval between shots, but they're too random. He grits his teeth.

I'm gonna get my head blown off.

He lifts his head to aim, but a bullet grazes the top of his head. Hans turns sharply and Victor flies into the back of the front seat.

"Agh," He feels for the crown of his head. A slight dampness registers at the tip of his fingers, "I can't get a clear shot. And I don't think even you can get that one."

But after a few more turns, the limo slides to a halt and the gears shift into park. They're in a space behind a tall corporate paradise of a building. "What are you doing?"

"Getting you a clear shot." Hans replies.

And it clicks. Victor kicks open his door and waits, counting in his head. He hears the screeching of wheels getting closer and closer, the rumbling of an engine shaking the asphalt beneath him. He smells something like burnt rubber, and he shoots.

The bullet hits the front tire of the first truck, which grinds to a stop on the sidewalk. The next truck crashes into its back, sending it spinning onto the road.

Victor slams the door shut before the truck comes tumbling a few feet from his window, crumpling from the impact. The driver of the final truck seems to have slammed the brakes, because his truck jerks forward to a stop, but too far ahead. The driver climbs out and fires a few rounds of his gun, missing every time. He walks out toward them, stumbling on his own feet. Victor imagines the dizziness the man must be experiencing, but takes it as a sign. He cocks his last round and takes aim. And the bullets keep flying.

He looks back at Marilyn. And the look in her eyes is almost enough to make him take his chances. Almost. But the bullets are still flying and sooner or later they'll land.

His finger tightens on the trigger.

A bullet tears into the man's chest, sending him tumbling onto the hood of the truck.

Victor's finger twitches on the trigger, the gun still ready to shoot. But the bullet never leaves the barrel. Wolff spins around to see the smoke still rising from the friction of the bullet in the gun held tightly in Hans's left hand.

"What—" He's not sure what he was about to ask, but his words are cut short by the sound of a door opening. A man in the passenger seat of the truck crawls out, a red streak of blood still marked at his temple. He hides behind the door and looks straight at them.

Victor takes aim again, but the man breaks into a run the other way. He feels the urge to shoot, but a hand holds the gun back.

Victor hadn't even seen Hans approach, but suddenly there he is, standing beside him, holding the barrel of his handgun.

A strange warmth fills Victor's chest. It makes him uncomfortable.

"If we've done it right," Hans says, "That last bullet will never have to leave the gun."

Victor nods. "If we've done it right," The passenger disappears behind a building, and Hans turns back into the gentle driver, sitting in front of the steering wheel, as if it had been a ghost of a memory rather than an actual exchange.

Victor lets himself back in the limousine and resists the urge to soothe his head. Hans starts the car and eases back onto the street like he's taking an evening stroll on their way to the airport for a beach vacation rather than driving away from a crash scene caused by the guards of a very bad person.

A very dead very bad person.

"What happened?" Marilyn finally takes the time to ask, "Did we get it?"

Victor reaches into the inner pocket of his jacket. "If this isn't it, then it doesn't exist." He draws out the small digital key.

Marilyn turns over the hard drive in her fingers. There's nothing spectacular about it, it looks like a normal key which opens a regular digital file, which is probably encrypted with thousands of different passwords, one following neatly after the other. But something about seeing it in person feels like a manifestation of their goals. It feels like a chance.

"It's smaller than I thought it'd be." She says casually.

Back on the road, Hand speeds through traffic, looking back every now and then to make sure they're not being followed, but stepping on the gas, not wanting to take their chances. In the distance, Victor can see the Astroport. Somehow, it feels like he's seeing it for the first time—the great white lights shining from every angle, enough to make you feel like you're flying through a star, the lanes of Navs arriving and departing, the constant rush of people like ants running to and from their colony—even though he had really been there earlier that day and several times before that running errands for Wren.

Victor remembers having read in a magazine that Urbis's Astroport is the biggest in the galaxy, spanning so and so units, twice as big as the one in Egeria. The Navs are the same, though. And the feel of dizziness on the terminal never varies, no matter what planet you're on. But to him it just means rest. To some degree.

"They won't stop coming for us." He says, more than anything to prepare himself.

"We can hide." Marilyn offers.

"We can't hide, they'll always find us, they have Wren's resources."

"Why would they look for us?"

"Because of that." He says pointing at the digital key.

"So what do we do?"

"Run. At least until we can get that somewhere safe."

"Where are we going?"

"I don't know yet."

"Well, it would be a good idea to find out before we get on a Nav."

"I bet it would, but—hold on." A glint had caught his eye a few moments earlier, but he had waved it off thinking it was just a glimmer from the Astroport, but now he sees it again, a small green glint of a light shining through his window. Victor traces the little beam of light to the top of a building. And then it disappears. A thrum of panic wells up in Victor's throat for a split second.

"NO, GET DOWN!"

And the world spins out of control, swallowed up by light and fire, glass and metal, and darkness.

Darkness like a sky with no stars.

Darkness.

24

The only thing he can hear is a ringing in his ears. His chest feels crushed, and his lungs struggle to find the strength to take a breath. He can feel more blood coming out of his head wound, but that's not what worries him. What worries him is the warmth spreading across his chest. His shirt is wet, he can feel it sticking to his stomach. But he can't feel his own body. And there's the ringing, a screaming in his ear.

Alive?

Everything feels so different than it did a moment ago. He remembers the feeling of triumph, but it all changed with the little green light shining through the window, shining on his chest. Everything changed. In a split second, it had disappeared, and the car swerved, roaring like a psychotic beast, and then it started spinning, rolling off the street, all the glass left shooting in every direction. A shard cutting his cheek.

He remembers Marilyn screaming, and then the stillness as the limo stops its violent turmoil.

Alive? How?

Again, he tries to breathe in, but the only thing that passes is a bitter taste of smoke and an unbearable heat. He feels its sting on his cuts and wounds. He urges his own arms to move, and lifts himself up, feeling the wetness on his chest. *Is this it? Am I dying?* He wonders. The ever-present fear looms over him like a mountain and brings its blow heavily on his chest. He turns to the window and looks into the building where the green beam was coming from, and he sees a blurry silhouette, and the light of three eyes. As suddenly as the image had appeared, it's gone.

Then he sees a bright orange light shining on his face. *Fire!* He wants to scream, but his voice is gone, nothing but a ghostly whisper.

He slides out from under whatever part of the limo was crushing him.

"Victor," He hears, a weak, hoarse whisper calling to him. A hand stretches out to him.

He reaches for Marilyn and takes her hand. Victor uses with all his strength to push the car off him, but even as he tries, he feels the futility of moving a mountain. And he feels the warmth pulling at his chest. He can almost hear death calling to him, but he grits his teeth and pushes in vain.

Can't be alive. How?

The pushing only makes the roof crush harder, as if it's laughing at him for trying, pushing back stronger. He can hear Marilyn struggling to crawl out, digging at the asphalt with her nails, the car groaning on top of them. She manages to shatter a window and a breath of fresh air drags through Victor's throat making him cough out a cloud of smoke.

"We have to go, Victor," She wheezes.

He tries to make out her face, but his sight is blurred by smoke and adrenaline.

"We have to go."

Victor concentrates what little strength he has left on willing his arms to move. Begging his arms to move. He reaches out toward the window, where Marilyn is already climbing out. She reaches in her hand for him. To drag him out of the fire. He knows she doesn't have the strength left to pull him out, but he takes her hand anyway and wriggles himself out, ignoring the pain of glass cutting against his skin.

The light of a thousand fluorescent stars shines on his face, he can hear crying, frantic muttering, ambulances in the distance and cops. Lots of cops. He can feel someone pulling him out from the ruins of the limo, from the warmth of the fire to the cold of the night. And he feels a different kind of pull. Back to the fire.

"Hans." He tries to say. No one answers. He feels another burst of adrenaline running through him. A surge of rage warming his chest. There's no time to think of the pain, of the bullet buried in his chest. Of the death approaching slowly, like a hornet hovering around him, poised for that deadly second sting.

He breaks free from the cop's grip and runs back toward the limo, stumbling with every step. The fire glares at him as he claws at the door, growling like a madman. The cop tries to pull him away again, but Victor yells and flails, pushing the cop out of the way, knocking him onto the floor. The door finally gives and creaks open halfway. Victor reaches in and manages to pull out a soot-stained, half-alive Hans.

The cop stands back up and pulls them out all the way. He doesn't take them back around, but instead sits on the edge of the sidewalk, soothing the back of his head as his comrades flank around the car, hands on their holsters and mumbling through their radios.

Hans flips on his side and coughs out a tiny puddle of blood. Victor slides back toward him and holds his head up. And he sees the blood branching out across Hans's chest, dampening the white linen. Victor feels his own chest, wet with nothing more than his own sweat and gasoline.

"Victor—"

"Hans," He finally manages to say, "I'm sorry. I'm sorry." He can feel the tears sliding down the sides of his eyes. The first he's felt in a while.

"Victor," Hans's eyes slide shut as he breathes out, "The bullet. Don't let it out."

"No, Hans, we'll get help, just don't—don't go." But Hans is taking a final breath, his chest rises and falls slower, until it stops. And there's silence. And it's torture. "Please, Hans." He whispers, holding the old chauffeur to his chest.

"Son, you need to step away from the car." One of the cops manages to say.

"No, I can't. I need to get to the Astroport." He says it feebly even as the cop signals to the others for backup.

Then he sees it. He sees the holster and the barrel. He sees the trigger. Right there, not even two feet away. The gun, bathed in orange firelight. The gun with one last shot. One last death. The power to take a life in a single device. A single action.

Alive?

Without knowing why, he reaches out for it, and wraps his fingers around its familiar grip. A new fear surges through him, and the gun takes control of his arm. It pulses like a heart. As if it has a heart of its own. It slides itself into the back of his pants, under his jacket. The cop comes back to him, taking him by the arms, lifting him away from the wreckage.

A couple of nurses lift Hans's body onto a gurney. They carry him into the ambulance.

The cop leads Victor between the burning hall of cops all the way to the ambulance, where Marilyn is wrapped in a blanket.

He feels a sting of shame seeing her face dirty with smoke and her hands trembling as she holds the blanket over her shoulders.

But he walks up to her and takes her hand. And he walks. Away from the ambulance. Marilyn looks at him confused, but stands up and follows his stride.

"Sir, stay in the ambulance." The cop says.

"Sir", not "son" anymore. They're afraid. Afraid of me.

He takes another step forward. Marilyn grips his hand tighter. Wolff walks toward the cop. And the cop takes a step back. Victor reaches his other hand behind his back and takes the gun, drawing a line in the air to bring it to the cop's chest. He feels the gaze of at least five more guns aimed right at his chest, ready to tear a bullet into him. Into his chest. Just like Hans.

He smiles. He doesn't know why, but he smiles. Ever so slightly.

"Sir, put the gun down or we will shoot!"

He feels Marilyn's hand loosening, and she's gone. She's not walking with him anymore.

Victor's smile fades. The adrenaline is gone. And he feels himself loosen his grip. He feels the presence of the last bullet in the gun. It still pulses. Whispers. *Fire. Just like they shot Hans, shoot them.*

And she's looking at him. Scared. And he knows what she's doing.

She's letting him see her fear.

"Victor," She says, like she's reading his mind, "They didn't kill Hans."

The gun still whispers. But her voice is louder.

It makes his hand shake. *I'm sorry, but isn't this who I am? It's all I know.*

"Victor, please." She whispers.

I'm sorry.

He exhales and feels the gun clatter to the ground, and the flames of the wreckage rise. The cops don't lower their weapons. They're looking at him the way they'd look at a criminal.

The cop walks up to him, handcuffs out, and starts citing a rehearsed Miranda warning.

"Anything you say can and will—"

"I want to make a call." He interrupts. Silently. The words are barely breathed out.

"What?"

"I want my phone call."

The cop looks at his colleagues. But he leads Wolff over to the ambulance. "There's the phone. You get one call, choose wisely."

Alive?

Victor types in a number. The phone rings several times.

There's a strange mix of hope and dread in the question ringing around his brain.

Alive?

And a hope that he won't pick up. But he does, and the receiver clicks.

"Who's this?"

Victor takes a breath before answering, "An old friend, sir."

There's silence on the other end for a while.

"You think you can hide from me?" The voice sounds weak and slurred, like talking to a quiet drunk.

"I think I can run. But I need your help to do it."

"Do you know who you're talking to?"

"You're gonna tell the cops to let me go. Or, eventually,

they'll find the file."

"I own the police, you can't blackmail me." The voice sounds like he's running out of breath.

A sharp stab of pain like an electric shock runs through Victor's head. He winces, but doesn't let it show. "Something like this would be a little hard to cover up, don't you think? Especially with all these people around. I may just scream it out before I go."

A curt laugh echoes in the receiver. "It doesn't matter if you go free, Victor. I'll find you anyway, wherever you hide."

There's a beat before Victor answers, looking at Marilyn. "I'll be waiting."

And there's a click as he hangs up. Victor smiles bitterly and puts the phone back. Then he turns to the cop, "I think you'll find everything is sorted out."

Just as he says it, the officer's radio wheezes out an order. "Let 'em go…"

"What? Let him go?" The cop asks back into the radio.

"Let 'em go…" The radio repeats, "Mr. Wren's orders."

The wind blows at them in the silence, moving the heat of the flames through the air. Victor feels the soot on his face smearing and drying. But he stares at the cop, waiting.

The officer glares at him, but signals a retreat.

Victor watches as the cops walk away crestfallen, back into their squad cars, gritting their teeth in defeat.

He turns to see Marilyn shivering despite the heat from the fire. In the most gentle voice he can summon, he says, "We should go."

"You were going to shoot him."

The words cut through skin and muscle into his chest. But he can't deny it. Does *he* even know? If it came to it, would he have pulled the trigger? He can feel his fists clench at the question. He wouldn't. And then the gun catches his eye, lying on the ground, the barrel staring back at him accusingly—that one bullet itching to escape.

"We should go."

Marilyn stands to walk away. Away from him. Away from the wreck of the limousine.

Away from the gun and the bullet.

The Astroport is just a short walk from the crash. Marilyn didn't look back at Victor the whole way. Victor walked after her, feeling a pit in his stomach as if someone was digging a hole inside of him. It reminds him of the feeling he got when he did his first job for Wren.

It was winter and the streets were filled with snow. He remembers the foggy frost of the morning chill blinding the view from the windows. But he could see a man sitting in a rocking chair, just barely visible, but clearly rocking in despair. He could only imagine the things going on in that man's mind. He can't remember his name now, but back then he didn't think he'd ever stop hearing it bouncing around in his mind. The man had gotten up only when the doorbell rang. His eyebrows tightened together seeing a seventeen-and-some-year-old standing at his door. Before he could tell Victor to "buzz off" he realized that this wasn't a friendly visit.

Victor can't remember exactly what happened next. He only remembers the man burying his face in his hands. And he remembers leaving with the same tightness in his stomach. Because he knew, despite his trying to convince himself, that what he was doing wasn't just harmless fair play. He was shoving a knife into people's lives and twisting the blade.

And Marilyn looked at him the same way that man had.

He'd had that same tightness in his stomach that night. The night he went to give his "condolences" to Marilyn on Wren's behalf. That tightness is the only thing that keeps him human.

The tap of his shoes wanders down the aisles of the Nav. He takes his seat beside Marilyn, but he can feel her recoil and shift when he sits down.

"Marilyn," He says.

She doesn't even turn to look at him, but he can see her eyes turning red.

So he doesn't look at her. He looks straight forward.

"I can't decide if I was going to shoot that cop. I think maybe I would have."

"Stop." She says weakly. Painfully.

"But I didn't. I didn't. I don't know exactly why, but I know it was because of you. This whole thing started with you. Maybe I'm not a good person. Maybe I'm just as bad as Wren. Maybe if it wasn't for you I would have become worse than him."

"Victor," She finally turns to look at him, her eyes begging him to stop talking. But the words are too heavy to hold them back now.

"I was sent to kill you, you know? That night, after she'd died. After Wren had killed her. He sent me to make sure you wouldn't leave the building so you'd go quietly."

He can hear the rumbling of the Nav taking off. So quickly. So rushed that you barely have time to get in and find your seat before you find yourself sliding off the platform and falling into the sky. Falling upwards. And he feels the fall.

He goes on.

"But, um, I couldn't do it. The same way I couldn't kill that cop."

Everything falls silent with the blackness of space. Victor can hear Marilyn breathing. Deciding.

And he finally looks at her. And there's still a smoke dryness in his voice. "Don't be afraid of me, Marilyn."

There's a beat before she speaks.

But she nods and clears her throat.

"You can't be him. You have to leave that behind. You can't be Wren anymore. We have to fix all this the right way."

There's a million words he could say. A million arguments he could make. But he doesn't.

He doesn't.

"We will."

Epilogue

The sky is gray. The sky is always gray at funerals. It's the world's way of sending you its condolences. *I'm sorry for your loss.* I can't bear how many times I've had to sit through the same conversation. But one more time won't make all that much difference.

"Hey, Pete, how are you holding up?" Some distant cousin named Sean walks up to me.

"I'm okay." But am I?

"I'm sorry—"

"For my loss?" And, for some reason, this time it hurts, "Yeah, me too."

There's an uncomfortable silence before the conversation continues the same way it has all day.

"How's your mom doing?"

"She's doing."

"Were you guys close?"

The question makes me smile, and I can't tell why, but memories of him race through my mind all at once. But one takes center stage. Me, about ten years ago, sitting on his lap listening to him tell stories about the people he worked with.

"He's the closest thing to a father I've ever had."

"How's that?"

"My biological father left when I was about four years old. My grandfather took care of my mother and me after that; until about two years ago. Then we moved out here."

My cousin smiles sadly. And then he says something I don't expect. Something no one has dared to ask.

"How did he die?"

Does he really not know?

My hand goes automatically to my pocket and wraps around something, and for a moment, I wonder what's in there.

"He crashed, driving his boss to the Port. He was shot in the chest."

"Oh." There it is. "I—uh—I'm sorry." He awkwardly turns to walk away. People always act awkward around families of murder victims. But I can't let him leave without telling him the whole story. It's out now and I can't take it back.

"They found a gun beside his car."

"Who—uh—whose was it?"

"His boss's. His boss who is now free, probably on his way to some party." I can feel a bitter taste as the words leave my mouth.

"Oh...You don't think he really shot him do you?"

And I look at him. I see how badly he wants to leave. "I don't care."

He keeps staring at me like he's watching an incoming storm.

"Well, I—uh—I hope they catch him." He says as he leaves.

I look back down at the gravestone at my feet and place the flowers I've been carrying beside it. They're already wilting from how hard I'd been strangling them without even noticing it.

"They won't catch him." I say to myself quietly. And I remember what's in my pocket.

My fingers glide over the object.

And I say a promise as my hand curls around it. I swear...

As my hand clasps the gun.
I swear…
The gun with one bullet.
Just for *him*.
I swear…
Just for Wolff.
"I swear I'll find you."

Also by Henri Leag

Explore some other works by Henri Leag.

Fate's Champion

Ames is home to those oppressed by the inhuman monarch residing there, the Arch. It is a sad land born from the ashes of a recent war, deep in the trenches of a poverty enforced by the Arch's Guard.

Fate has chosen a champion to save the world. Now, Abraham Skyfall must fight to find the truth behind the Arch's lies and free the people from the machine's rule.